BROKE[N]

Elizabeth glimpsed a shiny black BMW pulling into the Wakefields' driveway. The car rolled to a stop, and a tall, familiar figure emerged from behind the wheel. With long strides, he hurried to the house. Then the doorbell rang.

Elizabeth paused for a second, but there was no point in attempting to slow her racing heart. It couldn't be done.

She opened the door. And there was Todd, not as suntanned as he was when he lived in California, but just as handsome.

"Liz!"

Elizabeth felt the blood rushing to her cheeks. "Come in!" she finally managed to say, stepping back into the hallway.

Todd entered, and for a second he stood there, looking down at her. Then he pulled her into his arms for a long, close hug. "Liz. I've missed you so much!"

"Todd," Elizabeth whispered. His embrace was wonderfully warm, strong, and familiar. Elizabeth nestled her face against his muscular chest, just where she always had.

Then the magical moment was over. Elizabeth stepped back, not wanting to admit how close she and Todd had just come to kissing. What had she been thinking of? *Jeffrey*, she reminded herself. *Jeffrey is your boyfriend now.*

Bantam Books in the Sweet Valley High Series
Ask your bookseller for the books you have missed

SWEET VALLEY HIGH

BROKENHEARTED

Written by
Kate William

Created by
FRANCINE PASCAL

BANTAM BOOKS
NEW YORK · TORONTO · LONDON · SYDNEY · AUCKLAND

RL 6, IL age 12 and up

BROKENHEARTED
A Bantam Book / September 1989

Sweet Valley High is a registered trademark of Francine Pascal.

Conceived by Francine Pascal

*Produced by Daniel Weiss Associates, Inc.,
27 West 20th Street, New York, NY 10011*

Cover art by James Mathewuse

ISBN 0-553-28156-9

Published simultaneously in the United States and Canada

Bantam Books are published by Bantam Books, a division of Bantam
Doubleday Dell Publishing Group, Inc. Its trademark, consisting
of the words ''Bantam Books'' and the portrayal of a rooster, is
Registered in U.S. Patent and Trademark Office and in other countries.
Marca Registrada. Bantam Books, 666 Fifth Avenue, New York,
New York 10103.

PRINTED IN THE UNITED STATES OF AMERICA

O   0 9 8 7 6 5 4 3 2 1

BROKENHEARTED

One

Elizabeth Wakefield opened one eye and peeked at the clock radio on her nightstand. It was early even for a school day—the alarm wouldn't sound for another half hour.

Go back to sleep, she told herself, pulling the fuzzy, cream-colored blanket back up around her ears.

Then Elizabeth remembered what had made her toss and turn all night. Todd Wilkins, her first love, was moving back to Sweet Valley!

Todd and Elizabeth had been a serious and devoted couple for ages, until he and his family moved from California to Vermont. Even though many months had passed, Elizabeth would never forget the special times she and Todd had shared. She had thought she would never get over the pain of saying goodbye to him.

Elizabeth sat up in bed. Reaching over to the

window, she pushed back the filmy curtains. Outside, the morning sun made the dewy tree leaves sparkle.

"It just can't be true," Elizabeth said out loud, flopping back onto her pillows. As she closed her eyes her head spun with memories. Todd had moved to Burlington and they promised to stay in close touch, visit each other whenever possible, remain true. . . . Then there was that fateful Christmas when Todd returned to Sweet Valley and fell in love with Suzanne Devlin, a beautiful family friend of the Wakefields' from New York City who was staying with them for the holidays . . .

It had hurt. Not just Todd's caring for someone else, but Elizabeth's own realization that *her* feelings for Todd had changed. Or had they? If they had, why was she feeling like *this*—so unsure and yet so excited—now?

Todd and I agreed that as long as we were apart we had to live our own separate lives, Elizabeth reminded herself. Todd was free to go out with other girls and Elizabeth to date other guys. She knew Todd was no longer seeing Suzanne, but by now there might be another girl in the picture. And she had Jeffrey . . .

Jeffrey French, the sweetest, most caring and considerate guy in the world. Jeffrey, whose love had made Elizabeth forget about Todd—at least, she had thought so. . . .

Elizabeth and Jeffrey had been going out for

some time. Elizabeth loved spending time with him. He had become a very important part of her life.

Unfortunately, she still had to break the news to Jeffrey. He wasn't at the party Friday night when Lila had dropped the bomb about Todd's return, and Elizabeth hadn't been able to tell him about it over the weekend because he had been away, visiting relatives. She had no idea what she would say to Jeffrey when she saw him, and she had been worrying about it all weekend. Todd was moving back to Sweet Valley, but that wasn't the whole story. Elizabeth knew it, and Jeffrey would know it, too.

With Todd back in Sweet Valley, would she still want to date Jeffrey? Were her feelings for Jeffrey as strong as the love she had shared with Todd? If she had to choose between them, would she choose Jeffrey—or Todd?

Just then Elizabeth's soul-searching was interrupted. Her bedroom door swung open and rebounded against the wall with a clatter. Elizabeth's twin sister, Jessica, came in and jumped onto Elizabeth's bed, nearly squashing her.

"Well, what are you going to do about Todd, Liz?" Jessica demanded, her eyes sparkling with curiosity. "What are you going to tell Jeffrey when you see him today?"

Despite her anxiety, Elizabeth couldn't help smiling. Trust Jessica to be bursting with the news simply because it *was* news! Not many things could get Jessica out of bed on a Monday morning before she was forcibly evicted.

3

Settling herself cross-legged on Elizabeth's bed, Jessica observed her sister. Jessica had never been crazy about Todd Wilkins. In her opinion Todd was dull, and Todd and Elizabeth as a couple had been even duller. They were so absorbed in each other that they might as well have been *married*! She thought Jeffrey was more fun, and just as cute as Todd. Although, lately, Jeffrey and Elizabeth had seemed pretty settled and boring, too. That was Elizabeth for you, Jessica thought, serious about everything. Clearly Elizabeth needed some intrigue and spice in her life. And with Todd moving back to Sweet Valley, it looked as if she was going to get it!

To Jessica spice and intrigue were what life was all about. You only lived once, after all. And even after sixteen years, Jessica refused to give up trying to bring her twin around to her own way of thinking.

As it was, the resemblance between them was mainly on the surface. Elizabeth was five foot six and slender—so was Jessica. Elizabeth had long, silky blond hair that fell to her shoulders—so did Jessica. Elizabeth's golden California tan made her blue-green eyes even more brilliant—so did Jessica's. But anyone who knew the Wakefields well could tell them apart in a flash.

The twin in the wild zebra-striped miniskirt had to be Jessica, while the twin in conservative khakis and a comfortable short-sleeved cotton shirt was bound to be Elizabeth. Elizabeth spent hours on homework every night, while Jessica could never even find her books because they were buried beneath piles of discarded clothing in her bedroom. Elizabeth planned for the future and dreamed of a career as a writer. Jessica lived for the moment, figuring the future would take care of itself.

They were identical in their loyalty and support of each other, though, and they often knew what each other was thinking. Now Jessica leaned forward and stared at Elizabeth. "You're not exactly jumping up and down about the prospect of Todd moving back," she observed. "Don't you want to see him again?"

"Of course I do!" Elizabeth tugged at the window shade, and it sprang up with a snap. "But it's not just a question of seeing him again. He's moving back for good. I just don't know what's going to happen."

"Oh, you mean because of Jeffrey. They'll have to fight for you, I guess. Like in the old days—a duel!" The idea clearly appealed to Jessica. She giggled. "Picture Todd and Jeffrey going at it with french fries in the Dairi Burger!"

Elizabeth swatted her sister with a pillow. "Be serious for once!" she said.

Jessica sobered up and adopted a solemn expression. "I *am* serious, Lizzie. I'm serious about wanting to know whether you're going to break up with Jeffrey and get back together with Todd."

Elizabeth couldn't bear the thought of breaking up with Jeffrey. But if it came down to a choice between him and Todd she wasn't sure what she'd do.

Maybe I won't have a choice, she thought. According to Winston Egbert, Todd had told him about the upcoming move weeks ago. So why hadn't she heard the news from Todd himself?

"I don't know, Jess. Besides, it's not just up to me," Elizabeth said slowly.

"Why not?" Jessica asked. "Todd's moving back to Sweet Valley. Obviously he'll want to date you again."

"I'm not so sure." Elizabeth toyed with the satin ribbon around the neck of her favorite stuffed bear. "I haven't gotten a letter from him in a month or more. We're still in touch, but—"

Jessica cut Elizabeth off with an impatient wave of her hand. "Letters don't mean anything," she declared. "We're talking about your true love, not any old pen pal!"

Elizabeth shook her head. Letters, or rather the lack of them, *could* mean something, she was sure. "Todd might have a girlfriend in Vermont," she pointed out to Jessica. "If he hasn't written to tell me his family's moving back to California, Todd must not want to go out with me again."

Shrugging, Jessica hopped off the bed. She paused to admire her reflection in Elizabeth's mirror on the way to the door. "You're crazy, Liz," she teased. "With a face like this, you don't have to worry! Of course Todd will fall back in love with you—like that!" Jessica snapped

6

her fingers. Then she put her hands on her hips. "Now, get out of bed or you'll make us both late for school!" she scolded.

Elizabeth giggled at Jessica's imitation of the warning she usually gave her sister on school mornings. "OK, OK. I'm up!" she insisted.

Alone again, Elizabeth slipped into her terry-cloth robe and neatly made her bed. She would be at school in an hour, meeting Jeffrey as usual at her locker before homeroom. She had to tell him about Todd, or someone else would. Rumors, true or false, traveled fast at Sweet Valley High.

Elizabeth wasn't looking forward to the conversation.

"Say something!" Elizabeth begged. She had expected Jeffrey to be surprised, but not speechless.

It wasn't the ideal place for a private talk. Beyond them, the entire Sweet Valley High student body was rushing through the halls on the way to homeroom. But at least Elizabeth had gotten the difficult words out.

Jeffrey cleared his throat and shifted his feet, his white leather hightops squeaking on the linoleum floor. Then he smiled crookedly. "Well, um, I guess I'll look forward to meeting Todd. I know his old friends think a lot of him. He must be quite a guy."

A wave of affection swept over Elizabeth. Trust Jeffrey to be so generous and mature!

7

Jeffrey and Todd had never met. The Wilkinses had moved to Vermont before Jeffrey's own family had sold their Oregon tree farm and come to Sweet Valley. If anything, however, Elizabeth imagined that that made Jeffrey's position more difficult. To him, Todd was just a lingering school legend—the popular, handsome Sweet Valley basketball star who had dated Elizabeth Wakefield.

Underneath Jeffrey's casual words, Elizabeth detected a hint of doubt and hurt. Of course he would *say* the polite thing, even if he felt completely different.

"Well, I thought you should know," Elizabeth said awkwardly. "I mean, Todd was—he and I—"

"I know." Jeffrey's green eyes were dark and serious. "You don't need to tell me *that!*"

What am I supposed to tell you, then? Elizabeth wondered. But, actually, she knew what Jeffrey wanted to hear. Now was the moment she should assure him that nothing and nobody could ever come between them. Now was the moment to whisper, "I love *you*, Jeffrey, only you."

But the words stuck in Elizabeth's throat. She couldn't honestly swear that Todd's return meant nothing to her. She didn't know *what* it meant, not yet.

Jeffrey forced a hearty laugh. "We're still on for a movie Saturday night, aren't we?"

"Of course we are!" Elizabeth leaned forward and gave him a quick kiss.

8

The warning bell rang, and they both jumped. "Time to get going," Elizabeth said, relieved. "We can talk about this more later, if you want."

"I think we should," he agreed. For a moment he held her gaze, then he bent down to brush her cheek with a gentle kiss. "See you at lunch, Liz."

"Bye." Elizabeth watched as Jeffrey faded into the crowd, weaving his way down the hall with a soccer player's grace. His blond head and his broad shoulders beneath the checked flannel shirt were so lovably familiar. Elizabeth fought a crazy desire to run after him and promise that they would be together forever.

But she wouldn't make a promise she couldn't keep. And Elizabeth had a sinking suspicion that her dilemma was just beginning. There was one thing of which she was certain, though. If she had to choose between Jeffrey and Todd, it would be the toughest decision she would ever have to make.

Two

"A chocolate shake sounds *great*," Elizabeth said to Enid Rollins on Wednesday afternoon. "I didn't realize I was starving till you brought up the subject of food!"

After spending a couple of hours after school in the newspaper room polishing up her latest "Eyes and Ears" column for *The Oracle*, Elizabeth had run into her best friend as she was walking out of the Sweet Valley High library. Enid, exhausted from cramming for an upcoming test, had suggested they take a break and head for the Dairi Burger.

The two girls pulled into the parking lot of the popular hangout, Elizabeth behind the wheel of the red Fiat she and Jessica shared.

"We'll find a table for two, and you can tell me how things are going with Jeffrey since you

10

talked about Todd, OK?'' Enid's wide-set green eyes were concerned and sympathetic.

Elizabeth smiled, grateful as always for Enid's friendship. As much as Elizabeth loved Jessica, she didn't often turn to her twin when she needed constructive advice. Jessica always *meant* well, but her farfetched schemes were usually better suited to movie scripts than real life. Enid, on the other hand, had a good sense of humor *and* a lot of common sense.

Right then a table for two and a quiet talk sounded great to Elizabeth. It would be a relief to talk things over with Enid, she thought. But the instant the two girls entered the Dairi Burger, they saw that privacy was out of the question.

''Liz!'' Jessica cried out cheerfully from a table near the jukebox, where she was sitting with their classmates Lila Fowler, Ken Matthews, Aaron Dallas—and Jeffrey. ''Over here!'' Jessica shouted. ''We've got plenty of room.''

Elizabeth and Enid exchanged a helpless glance. There was nothing to do but join the party.

Jeffrey, his hair still wet from a post-soccer-practice shower, scooted his chair over to make room for Elizabeth. His welcoming smile and the arm he put around her shoulders were easy and warm. Elizabeth crossed her fingers and hoped the subject of Todd Wilkins wouldn't come up to ruin the carefree mood.

But no sooner had Elizabeth taken a seat and

11

ordered her milk shake than Lila announced, "Liz, *you'll* be interested in *this.*"

Lila's insinuating tone was as subtle as a squad car siren. Elizabeth had a feeling she could guess what Lila would say next. *Todd, again! And in front of Jeffrey.* But, of course, Lila enjoyed making people uncomfortable. It was one of her hobbies.

Tossing her long light brown hair over one shoulder, Lila rested her elbows on the wood-topped table, taking care not to snag her silk blouse. "I have inside information courtesy of my father, whose microchip company, as you know, does business with Varitronics," Lila began. "When Winston told us Todd's father was being transferred back to Sweet Valley, he neglected to mention the fact that Mr. Wilkins has been named the new *president* of Varitronics! Isn't that fabulous?"

"President!" repeated Jessica, awed.

President, Elizabeth thought, equally impressed, but not willing to show her feelings. She was eager to learn more but knew better than to encourage Lila.

"Yes, president of Varitronics," Lila continued, her brown eyes gleaming. "That will put Todd's father in the *Fortune* Five Hundred along with *my* father."

Enid rolled her eyes, and Elizabeth stifled a giggle. Lila was such a snob! George Fowler, easily one of the wealthiest men in Southern

12

California, spoiled his daughter to compensate for the fact that he rarely spent time with her. Jessica's love-hate relationship with Lila had always mystified Elizabeth. One minute the two would be happily mall-hopping together, and the next, Jessica would insist that she was never speaking to Lila again. As far as Elizabeth could tell, this cycle was repeated at least every other week.

"I'm sure Mr. Wilkins worked very hard to earn such a big promotion," Elizabeth commented.

Lila shrugged. "Whatever. But guess what? The Wilkinses have bought a *mansion*, right down the street from Fowler Crest! Todd and I are going to be *neighbors*!"

While the others discussed this latest tidbit Elizabeth stole a short moment alone with her thoughts. President of Varitronics? A mansion near Fowler Crest? If Lila had the story right, it was a remarkable one.

When Todd's family lived in Sweet Valley before, they had been comfortably well-off, much like the Wakefields. But as a corporate president, Mr. Wilkins would obviously be making a much higher salary. Everyone knew what Lila's neighborhood was like. The residences were all as sprawling and opulent as Fowler Crest, a Spanish-style mansion complete with a fountain, a huge swimming pool, and sculptured grounds.

13

As hard as she tried, Elizabeth couldn't picture down-to-earth Todd in that setting. Todd had always been the first to roll his eyes at Lila's pretensions or to tease another rich Sweet Valley friend, Bruce Patman, whenever he started boasting. But now it appeared that Todd was going to share Lila and Bruce's elevated social status. Elizabeth wondered if it would change him.

"Well, I got a letter from Todd yesterday," Ken Matthews, the handsome blond captain of the football team, announced. "And get this— his folks signed him up to go to that really snobby private school, Lovett Academy. So Todd won't be sinking baskets for the Sweet Valley Gladiators anymore."

Elizabeth stared blankly at Ken. He and Winston both had received letters from Todd—and she hadn't. She bent her head to sip her milk shake, hoping to hide her distress.

But Lila was too sharp to miss Elizabeth's reaction. "I'm sure Todd has written to *you*, Liz," she said sweetly. "What news do you have to pass along?"

"Well, actually, I haven't heard from Todd too recently," Elizabeth said, her breezy tone forced.

"I *see*," Lila purred.

"Well, it'll be great to have Todd back," Enid observed, tactfully bringing the subject to a close. "Whether he's playing basketball for us or not!

Speaking of sports, what do you guys think your chances are against El Carro High on Saturday?"

At Enid's question Jeffrey and Aaron, both starters on the soccer team, began discussing that weekend's game. Jessica and Lila fell to anticipating the upcoming sale at Lisette's, an exclusive boutique at the Valley Mall. Elizabeth, meanwhile, listened with half an ear as Ken complained good-naturedly about the English paper they both had to write for Mr. Collins's class. She was too distracted by her own thoughts to focus clearly on Ken's words.

Her mind was in a whirl. Not only was Todd moving back to Sweet Valley, but he was also returning as the son of the new Varitronics president. He would practically be a celebrity! Todd had always been fun, intelligent, and popular. Now that he was rich, he would probably be even more popular than before.

Elizabeth nodded at a remark of Ken's and sipped her chocolate shake, but she was still thinking about Todd. Maybe it was no wonder she hadn't heard from him! Maybe he wanted to come back to Sweet Valley and date a lot of girls. Plenty of girls—wealthy, beautiful ones like Lila—were bound to chase after him now.

Maybe I was wrong to worry that I'd be forced to choose between Jeffrey and Todd, Elizabeth realized, not sure whether she felt relieved or disappointed. *It sounds like there will be a lot more competition for Todd's attention. Maybe I won't even be in the running!*

"We can beat them by at least four goals," Aaron Dallas stated after the four girls had left the Dairi Burger. He looked at his best friend for confirmation. "Don't you think so, French?"

"What?" Jeffrey shook his head, realizing he barely knew what Aaron was talking about.

"Four goals," Aaron repeated patiently. "I think we can beat El Carro by at least four goals on Saturday."

"Sure," Jeffrey hastened to agree. But secretly he thought he didn't care if they beat El Carro by four or lost by four hundred. What was winning or losing a game, he thought, compared to winning or losing Elizabeth?

The girls had left the Dairi Burger a quarter of an hour ago, Elizabeth and Jessica offering to drop Enid at home and Lila taking off alone in her lime-green Triumph.

Jeffrey had walked Elizabeth to her car. Her goodbye kiss was sweet and lingering, and as always, she had promised to call him that night after dinner. Even so, Jeffrey couldn't feel at ease. When Lila had brought up Todd's name earlier, it had been only too obvious that Elizabeth's feelings about her former boyfriend were far from neutral.

As Aaron and Ken discussed the similarities between soccer and football offensive strategies,

Jeffrey thought about the whole Todd-Elizabeth question. When Elizabeth broke the news about Todd to him, she had been a little nervous—understandably, Jeffrey conceded. But in addition to nervousness, he had detected an uncharacteristic evasiveness. He suspected that Elizabeth, who always shared her thoughts and feelings with him, was holding something back.

Now, two days after that initial conversation, Elizabeth had yet to deny that Todd's return would affect her relationship with Jeffrey. Granted, Jeffrey hadn't come right out and demanded such a denial. But the unspoken question hung in the air between them, as plain to Elizabeth, Jeffrey was sure, as it was to him.

What sort of threat was Todd Wilkins? When Jeffrey first started seeing Elizabeth, he knew there had been a serious romance in her past. But Jeffrey had never felt Todd's memory come between them—until now. And now it wasn't just Todd's memory that was troublesome—it was Todd himself, who would be back in town any day. And not only that, but he had a new and improved image. Apparently he *used* to be a nice ordinary guy—a regular Sweet Valley High junior. Sure, he was a basketball star and all that, but he wasn't Superman. Now, though, Todd's dad had become a corporate president, and Todd would have an affluent life-style that impressed even Lila Fowler.

Of course, Jeffrey knew Elizabeth wasn't con-

17

cerned with superficial qualities such as money and status. But she had fallen in love with Todd once before. Jeffrey just couldn't help viewing the new high-society angle as frosting on an already impressive cake.

"We're outta here," Ken announced, hooking a thumb toward the Dairi Burger door. Aaron was already on his feet, one arm wrapped around a bulging take-out bag.

As Jeffrey trailed his friends to the parking lot, he decided there was only one way to learn more about his rival for Liz's affection.

"So, tell me a little about this Todd Wilkins guy, anyway," he said casually. "What's he like?"

"Todd? He's great!" Ken, a close friend of Todd's, clearly was psyched about seeing his old pal again. "A lot of fun to hang out with, although he does have a serious side. He was always a pretty good student. Active. You know, the student government type. Just don't ever let him talk you into a foul shot contest. He can sink ten in a row from half court!"

"Todd's a regular guy," Aaron added. "You'll like him. Everybody does."

Jeffrey wasn't so sure. Ken and Aaron talked as if it hadn't occurred to them that there could be tension between Jeffrey and Elizabeth because Todd was coming back to town. Or were they and the rest of the gang secretly feeling sorry for him, figuring it was only a matter of days before Elizabeth's name would once again be linked with Todd's?

Don't be so paranoid! Jeffrey ordered himself as he slid into the passenger seat of Ken's white Toyota. But he couldn't help thinking that if it came to an all-out contest for Elizabeth's love, he would lose.

Three

Miss Elizabeth Wakefield, the envelope read in extremely familiar, slightly messy handwriting.

On Friday after school, Elizabeth had parked the Fiat in the driveway and walked toward the front of the house to get the mail. Now she was frozen in front of the mailbox, holding the letter from Todd in one hand.

Elizabeth studied the envelope. It looked as if it had been around the world. There were numerous creases and smudges and at least three postmarks on it. The earliest cancellation was dated three weeks earlier.

Todd did write to me, Elizabeth realized, her heart flooding with a sudden intense happiness. But the post office had had trouble deciphering the hastily scribbled address, and the letter had been sent elsewhere first.

Elizabeth sat down on the front steps. With

trembling fingers she carefully opened the letter. Inside were two sheets of lined notebook paper, filled with writing on both sides.

"Dear Elizabeth," the letter began. To Elizabeth's surprise her eyes momentarily clouded, and a tear crept down one cheek. "Don't be so sentimental, you goof!" she chided herself.

Dear Elizabeth,

I know it's been a while since my last letter, but I thought I'd wait until I had some really big news. You'll never guess what it is, Liz, so I'll just come right out and tell you. Maybe you'd better sit down first! I'm moving back to Sweet Valley!

The words on the paper, written by Todd's very own hand, had as powerful an effect on Elizabeth as if she were learning the news for the first time. Her heart skipped a beat, and her hand, clutching the page, was damp.

No kidding. I'm still in shock about it myself, to tell you the truth! The more I think about it, though, the more excited I get. Sure, I've come to really like Burlington. I'll miss the friends I've made here. But Vermont's not home, not like California.

A yellow Buick pulled out onto the street from the driveway next door. Elizabeth looked up at the sound of its horn. Mrs. Beckwith, a neighbor of the Wakefields', waved cheerily to her. Elizabeth waved back, then got to her feet and carefully refolded the letter. She decided to go inside rather than read her personal letter in front of the rest of the world!

The house was quiet—and empty. Elizabeth wandered past the airy living room, down the hallway, and into her father's wood-paneled study. Curling up on the sofa, she continued reading Todd's letter.

This is how it all happened. My father has been managing Varitronics' Burlington office, and I guess they're pretty pleased with his work. So when the current president of the company, Mr. Kane, takes over in a few weeks as chairman of the board and C.E.O., my dad will become the new president! Mom and I are really proud of him. Anyway, I wanted you to be the first to know. If all goes well—we're selling the place here and Dad's closing a deal on a house in Sweet Valley—we'll be back in town on the fifteenth of next month, for good. Feel free to spread the word! I can't wait to see the old gang again.

"Spread the word!" Elizabeth said out loud, smiling in spite of herself. "Sorry, Todd. Lila already did that for me!" Then she glanced back a sentence or two. The fifteenth—that was *this* Sunday! Only two days away.

When Todd mailed the letter, Elizabeth thought, he probably believed he was giving her plenty of time to adjust to the idea. He couldn't have guessed the letter would be delayed and that she would hear the news in such a roundabout fashion.

There's one thing I'm not too happy about. I won't be back at Sweet Valley High. There's a private school in Cedar Springs called Lovett Academy. Have you heard of it? Well, I'm going there instead. It was my parents' idea, and I'll tell you, I wasn't interested at first. But my dad is convinced that going to a prep school will help me get into a good college. Maybe he's right. Anyway, I'm sure Lovett will be fine, but I'll miss being at Sweet Valley High with Winston and Ken and the guys—and you.

Elizabeth certainly had heard of Lovett Academy, the prestigious school about forty minutes from Sweet Valley. The distance to Cedar Springs and the fact that Sweet Valley had a very strong public school system deterred other well-to-do Sweet Valley students, such as Lila and Bruce, from attending Lovett.

But school—that's not what matters to me. Liz, it's been a long time. Did you ever think I'd move back to Sweet Valley and we'd have a chance to be together again? I didn't. And now it's happening. I can't wait to see you again. You've never stopped being my best friend. Thousands of miles couldn't change that. There are so many things I want to say to you! But they don't belong in a letter. They'll have to keep till I can say them in person. I'm only afraid you won't want to hear them. Liz, I know you're seeing someone. I'm not, not since my relationship with Suzanne ended. So maybe our perspectives about this are going to be different. I have to tell you this much now, though. I've never stopped caring for you. No girl has ever meant as much to me as you did—as you still do. I'm only wondering: Where do I stand with *you*?

The letter slipped from Elizabeth's fingers. Todd wasn't dating anyone in Vermont! He still cared for her. She reread the final line. "I'm only wondering: Where do I stand with *you*?"

Elizabeth heaved a deep, shaky sigh. She couldn't deny that it made her feel light-headed just knowing that Todd still had feelings for her. But it was an unsettling feeling, too. It proved that she still had a lot of emotions invested in her relationship with Todd—more than she'd been willing to admit to herself.

Elizabeth could no longer ignore the dilemma that was facing her. The past—her love for Todd—was about to collide with the present—her relationship with Jeffrey. As for the future . . .

She would have to make up her mind soon.

"I've browned the hamburger and sautéed the onion," Enid announced. "Now what?"

Elizabeth glanced at the recipe. "Add the tomatoes and tomato paste," she instructed. She gave a light toss to the egg noodles she was draining in a colander. "Then add some salt and freshly ground pepper, and Chef Rollins's half of the casserole will be done!"

After reading Todd's letter, Elizabeth had needed someone to talk to. She had called Enid, and her friend stopped over to help make dinner. Since both their parents worked, Elizabeth and Jessica took turns preparing the evening meal—theoretically, anyway. Jessica had a habit of disappearing in the late afternoon, whether it was for a legitimate reason such as cheerleading practice or some trumped-up excuse. Tonight, however, Elizabeth didn't mind making dinner. It was nice to have the cozy, Spanish-tiled kitchen to herself and Enid.

They layered the noodle and meat sauce mixtures in a baking dish, then placed the dish in the oven. Elizabeth set the timer and then collapsed in a chair at the kitchen table.

Enid took an open bag of pretzels out of the cupboard and ate one. "I can't believe Todd'll be here on Sunday!" she said after munching for a moment.

"Tell me about it!" Elizabeth took a pretzel.

25

"I don't know what to wear, what to say, how to act—help!"

"Well, how do you *feel*?" Enid asked. "Did the letter make things any clearer?"

"You mean about how I feel for Todd compared to how I feel for Jeffrey?" When Enid nodded, Elizabeth shrugged her shoulders. "Not really. I used to *dream* of the day Todd and I could be together again. But Todd and I can't turn the clock back to before his family moved to Vermont. At least, *I* can't."

"Jeffrey," Enid said, snapping a pretzel in half with a sigh.

"Jeffrey," agreed Elizabeth.

"What does *he* think about all this?"

Elizabeth frowned. "He's not exactly thrilled. Basically, he doesn't know what to think because he's not getting clear signals from me. Because *I* don't know what I think!"

Enid reached over to pat her friend's hand. "You've just got to be patient—all three of you. Todd's a sensitive guy, Liz. He'll give you the time and space you need to figure things out. And I'm sure Jeffrey understands this isn't easy for you. If he loves you, he should be able to deal with a week or so of uncertainty."

Enid's calming words made a lot of sense. "But what about *me*?" Elizabeth asked. "What should I say this weekend when I see Todd? I wouldn't want him to get the wrong idea, to think either that I'm ready to drop everything for him *or* that I don't care at all."

"I don't think you can plan a speech or anything," Enid said. "You'll know when you see him how to act! Just take things one step at a time."

One step at a time. . . . Elizabeth was pretty sure she could handle that much.

"Pretzels, *yum!*" Jessica ran into the kitchen and headed straight for the open bag on the counter. "All those handsprings have made me *ravenous!*" she exclaimed.

Elizabeth laughed. As always, Jessica's timing was perfect. She arrived just as the casserole went into the oven, not a minute sooner!

"How was practice today, Jess?" she asked.

Jessica pulled up a chair and straddled it. "OK," she answered, her voice muffled as she wiggled out of her pink sweatshirt. "We've got the pyramid down pat for the next game. What are you two gabbing about?"

While Jessica devoured half the bag of pretzels, Elizabeth filled her in on the details of Todd's letter. "So Enid came over to play Dear Abby and give me advice," she concluded.

"What did you decide to do?" Jessica asked, going over to the copper-colored refrigerator to get a can of diet soda.

"I decided to be patient with myself," answered Elizabeth. "I'll welcome Todd back to Sweet Valley, and we'll go from there. The most important thing is to renew our friendship. As for anything more, I don't know if he'll want it, and I don't know if I'll want it."

It was plain Jessica was dissatisfied with this strategy. Snapping the tab on the can, she adopted a serious tone. "I think you'd be making a big mistake, Liz, if you didn't get back with Todd right away on Sunday."

"Get back with *Todd*?" Elizabeth raised her eyebrows. "Didn't you tell me just this morning at breakfast to stick with Jeffrey?"

Jessica did recall saying something along those lines, but that was before she'd had a chance to consider this new angle on Todd. In Jessica's mind there really wasn't a contest anymore. Nice as he was, Jeffrey was just Jeffrey—while Todd was now a *somebody*. Todd would be attending Lovett Academy in posh Cedar Springs!

Jessica had heard all about Lovett from Lila, who knew a Lovett girl from the country club. It sounded like heaven on earth. All the boys were handsome, smart, and *rich*. They dressed well, and they knew how to treat a girl.

If Elizabeth got back together with Todd, she would probably start spending some time with him at Lovett. And Jessica would join them. She had absolutely no qualms about playing the part of third wheel. After all, she would only tag along enough to find a fourth wheel—her very own Lovett man!

"I don't remember what I said at breakfast," Jessica now declared, making it sound as if breakfast had occurred sometime in the last century. "If Todd comes back to Sweet Valley and wants to get involved with you, I think you'd be crazy

28

to say no. He's not going to wait around, Liz. *Action*, that's what it's all about!" she argued.

Elizabeth groaned. "Action? Jess, we're not talking about a football game, you know!"

Jessica folded her arms across her chest. "We're talking about life, and you have to sprint in order to win in life, too," she pointed out. "I'm only trying to help, Liz. Really, I have *your* best interests at heart."

Your best interests—and mine! Jessica thought.

Four

Elizabeth hadn't known what the word *nervous* meant until this moment. It was late Sunday morning, and she was sitting tensely on the living room couch, trying to remain calm and convince herself that everything was under control.

An hour earlier Todd had called from a pay phone at the airport. He said he was on his way to the new house with his parents but would stay only long enough to help carry in the suitcases. Then he'd hop into the new car his dad had bought for him and drive over to the Wakefields'.

Elizabeth hadn't been able to eat a bite of the delicious Sunday brunch her father had prepared. Eggs Benedict and fresh-squeezed orange juice might as well have been stale bread and water, as far as she was concerned.

Elizabeth stood up and nervously straightened her jade-green twill skirt. Then she adjusted the collar of her white silk blouse. Putting a hand to her throat, she felt the gold locket on the chain around her neck. Usually she wore a gold lavaliere, a gift from her parents on her sixteenth birthday. But today she was wearing the locket that Todd had given her a long time ago. Inside it was his picture.

Elizabeth tucked the locket under her blouse and out of sight. It had been months since she'd worn it. When she began dating Jeffrey, the locket was relegated to the bottom drawer of her little jewelry box with other items from the past. Why had she put it on this morning? Elizabeth wasn't sure. Nostalgia, she guessed.

"Psst!" Elizabeth jumped at the noise. Jessica was sticking her head around the doorway. "Need some company? Maybe it'd be better if I waited with you. I'll distract you from being nervous. Then when Todd gets here, I promise I'll leave—"

"Thanks, but no thanks!" Elizabeth wanted to be alone when she saw Todd, and she didn't trust Jessica to take off when there was a chance something exciting might happen. "Mom and Dad are out back by the pool. Why don't you leave *now* and join them?"

"I get the hint. Two's company . . ." With a knowing grin, Jessica disappeared. A few minutes later, Elizabeth glimpsed a shiny black BMW pulling into their driveway. The car rolled to a stop, and a tall, familiar figure emerged from behind the wheel. With long strides, he hurried to the house. Then the door bell rang.

Elizabeth paused for a second, her hand on the doorknob. But there was no point attempting to slow her racing heart. It couldn't be done.

She opened the door. And there was Todd, not as suntanned as he was when he lived in California, but just as handsome.

"Liz!"

Elizabeth felt the blood rushing to her cheeks, but for the life of her she couldn't move her tongue to speak. "Come in!" she finally managed to breathe, stepping back into the hallway.

Todd entered and for a second stood looking down at her. Then he pulled her into his arms for a long, close hug. "Liz. I've missed you so much!"

"Todd," Elizabeth whispered. His embrace was wonderfully warm, strong, and familiar. Elizabeth nestled her face against his muscular chest just where she always had. She felt his chin brush her hair.

Then the magical moment was over. Todd gently released her and stepped back. This time his smile was reserved, awkward.

We can't take anything for granted, Elizabeth thought. *Things aren't the same. There's so much I don't know about him and he doesn't know about me. Friendship or romance, we have to start at the beginning again.*

"Did you have a nice trip?" she asked.

They walked over to the couch and sat down side by side, leaving a little space between them. "Oh, sure," Todd said, running a hand through his curly brown hair. "Nonstop from Boston, and we gained three hours along the way. Can't beat that!"

Elizabeth nodded, fidgeting with a throw pillow. Another shy silence fell between them. Then they both started talking at once.

Elizabeth laughed. "You first!"

Todd shrugged his broad shoulders. "I was just going to say—" He paused to clear his throat. "You're as beautiful as ever, Elizabeth."

"Oh. Thanks." She blushed. "You look great yourself! You're still—tall!"

They both laughed at her observation. "I don't know what I'm saying," confessed Elizabeth, lowering her eyes. "It's been a long time. I'm so happy to see you, Todd! I can't seem to find the right words, though."

"Me, either," Todd assured her. "But that's OK. We don't have to say everything today. We don't have to say *anything*. It's enough for me just to look at you. To be with you."

He reached out his hand to give hers a gentle squeeze. Elizabeth squeezed back, grateful. Then she withdrew her hand, nervously putting it to her throat to toy with the gold chain. Without thinking, she pulled the locket out from under the collar of her blouse.

Todd immediately recognized it. His eyes

brightened. "My locket—you're wearing it," he said. "Elizabeth, does that mean . . . ?"

Elizabeth released the necklace, her hand suddenly cold. Maybe it had been a mistake to wear it. Every word, glance, and gesture in this first meeting with Todd seemed to be loaded with significance.

"It doesn't mean anything," she said lightly, struggling to keep her tone casual. "I only thought I'd wear it to welcome you back."

If Todd was disappointed, he didn't show it. "Well, thanks." Then he laughed. "I'm sorry, Liz. Look at me, jumping to conclusions! I just got carried away, I guess. I know about . . . but I still wish—" He hesitated, his dark eyes growing serious. "All I want is to see you now and then, to spend some time with you."

"Of course! I want that, too." Elizabeth put her hand on his arm. "Todd . . ."

Suddenly they weren't sitting a couple of feet apart on the sofa anymore. They were right beside each other. And Todd's face was very close to hers.

Elizabeth jumped to her feet, not wanting to recognize how close she and Todd had just come to kissing. What had she been thinking of? *Jeffrey*, she reminded herself. *Jeffrey is your boyfriend now.*

"Jessica is dying to say hello to you, Todd," Elizabeth stammered. "I know she's lurking around here somewhere, waiting to pounce—"

As if on cue, Jessica popped into the living

34

room. "Hey, Wilkins!" She grabbed Todd in a bear hug and he whirled her around, making her squeal with laughter.

It was all Elizabeth could do to keep the cheerful smile on her face. There were so many emotions whirling around inside her that it hurt.

And Todd had only been back in Sweet Valley for an hour!

"Well, Todd, we're happy to officially welcome you, and of course your parents as well, back to the community," Mr. Wakefield said heartily at dinner Wednesday night. The handsome, dark-haired man raised his wineglass. "We only wish we were also welcoming you back to the Sweet Valley High basketball team! Cheers, everyone!"

As Elizabeth lifted her glass of milk, she caught Todd's eye, and a private, amused glance passed between them. Before the meal Elizabeth had bet Todd her father would make a corny but sincere toast in his honor. Todd now owed her a double-dip cone at Casey's Ice Cream Parlor.

"Any flavor you want," he promised Elizabeth in a low voice.

"What was that?" Jessica asked.

"Oh, nothing," Elizabeth said airily. "Please pass the bread, Jess."

Todd and Elizabeth had talked on the phone a couple of times since his arrival, but this was the first time they had seen each other since their initial reunion. It wasn't easy to get together, since Todd attended a different school and often did not make it back to Sweet Valley until the evening.

When Elizabeth's mother suggested that Todd join the family for dinner, Elizabeth had quickly agreed. She thought it would be a perfect opportunity to spend some time with him in a neutral situation. There was nothing romantic about eating dinner chaperoned by her parents.

So, in an effort to be completely aboveboard, Elizabeth had told Jeffrey that Todd was coming over for dinner. She hadn't worried, because she figured there was no reason for Jeffrey to take offense or feel threatened.

But Jeffrey knew her too well. She knew he had sensed the change in her. She couldn't hide it; she had been distracted and dreamy since Sunday. To Jeffrey "dinner with the family" probably made it sound as though Todd was being ushered back into his old position as her boyfriend. Elizabeth had spent the better part of lunch period assuring Jeffrey it meant nothing of the sort, but he had been very upset, and so now she was upset. It tore at her heart to know she was causing Jeffrey pain. She felt so guilty that she couldn't even eat. She managed to swallow a few forkfuls of salad, but the chicken divan on her plate remained untouched.

Jessica's appetite was unaffected, however, and so was her curiosity. "I'm dying to hear all about Lovett Academy, Todd! What's the campus like? What are the *students* like?"

Todd chuckled, and Elizabeth rolled her eyes. It was obvious to everybody that by "students" Jessica meant *boys*.

"The campus is beautiful," he answered amiably. "It looks almost like a college campus. There are lots of old ivy-covered buildings, and there's a big quad in the middle where everyone hangs out."

"And the students?" Jessica prompted.

Todd shrugged. "The students are just like students anyplace else."

Jessica's face fell. Mr. Wakefield laughed. "Looks like that was the wrong answer," he remarked.

Todd winked at Elizabeth. "OK, Jess, I'll admit it. Lovett's a lot different from Sweet Valley High in every way!"

Todd went on to describe some of his new acquaintances. Of course he was tactful, but Elizabeth could read between the lines. Lovett students, boys and girls, clearly *were* different. It sounded as if most of them were children of wealthy businessmen or famous movie directors. Needless to say, Jessica ate up every detail.

Later, as Mrs. Wakefield served fresh-baked peach pie topped with homemade whipped cream, she asked Todd about his parents' plans to redecorate the new house. Todd obligingly gave her a quick room-by-room rundown, but after a minute or two Elizabeth lost count of the rooms! There was a parlor, a family room, a den, a library, and there seemed to be at least twelve bedrooms. The only thing the new house didn't have was a silly name like Fowler Crest! Maybe it was only a matter of time before it became known as Wilkins Estate.

Jessica couldn't tolerate this conversation about wallpaper and carpeting for long. Soon she had Todd back on the subject of Lovett. And as Todd tossed off strange names—like Courtney, Sheffield, April—Elizabeth pictured him fitting in easily with this new, glamorous crowd.

The situation was growing more complicated by the minute. With his new mansion and private school status, it wasn't just a question of how Todd would fit back into Elizabeth's world. How would *she* fit into *his*? she wondered.

"I guess we'll have to skip the ice cream tonight." Todd patted his stomach. "There's no room in here even for one scoop of heavenly hash! By the way, Liz, thanks for having me over. It was great to hang out with you and your folks again."

He and Elizabeth were sitting in the backyard by the pool. A balmy night breeze blew through Elizabeth's loose hair. Pushing a wisp out of her eyes, Elizabeth smiled. "You know you're welcome any time, Todd. Only I can't promise my dad will go to the trouble of making a toast again!"

Todd laughed. "OK by me. It felt a little funny being the center of attention, anyway. But other than that it was just like the old days."

Elizabeth didn't know how to respond to that. She couldn't help feeling that it wasn't like the old days—not at all. Back then she had never questioned her love for Todd.

"Liz, look at me," Todd pleaded.

Elizabeth turned her head to face him. "Hmm?"

"You were awfully quiet during dinner. Is something on your mind?"

There sure is, Elizabeth wanted to say. *There are a thousand things on my mind.*

But she just smiled. "Was I quiet? I guess I was. But *you're* the one with all the exciting stories to tell, about Lovett and all."

"You know, Liz, Lovett wasn't my idea." Todd sat forward, resting his elbows on his knees. "I'd give anything to be at Sweet Valley with you and the rest of the gang. But I can't let my parents down."

"I understand," Elizabeth said softly.

"I'm not sure you do," Todd told Elizabeth. "You've got to believe the only thing that'll make it bearable will be coming home at night—and having friends like you."

"Friends like me," Elizabeth echoed.

"Friends," Todd repeated. It was almost as if they both were trying to convince themselves that that was all they were to each other. "Elizabeth, I won't pretend with you. I'd like us to be more than friends. I understand, though. The time's just not right. But I'll wait for you. Just let me believe there's some hope for us."

Elizabeth's feelings of guilt returned. Now she was making two boys wait for her to make up her mind! "But, Todd," she protested, "it's asking too much of you, when I can't—"

"No, it's not," Todd insisted. "I can wait. It's worth it to me."

"Thanks, Todd," Elizabeth practically whispered.

Todd looked at his watch. "I should really be heading home," he said, rising to his feet. "I don't want to cheat you out of that ice-cream cone, though. How about Saturday, before the party at Winston's?"

"Oh, I'm—I have—other plans," Elizabeth said awkwardly. She and Jeffrey already had a date to go to the party together.

"All right. Another time, then," Todd promised her. He seemed to understand.

They walked around the house to the BMW, Todd with one arm lightly around Elizabeth's shoulders. At the car he gave her a quick hug and then dropped his arm. "There *will* be another time, won't there, Liz?" he asked.

Elizabeth nodded. "Yes, there will. Good night, Todd," she said warmly.

" 'Night, Liz." Todd got into the car, started the engine, and then backed down the driveway to the street.

As Elizabeth watched him drive away she

couldn't help wishing things were different between her and Todd, that they were more than friends, just as he'd said. It didn't seem natural not to kiss him good night.

But she didn't know if that was just a passing impulse or the way she really felt. She was sure she felt just as strongly about Jeffrey, if not more so.

How was she supposed to know what to do?

Five

"Oh, Jeffrey, they're beautiful!" Elizabeth exclaimed, reaching out to accept the bouquet of red long-stemmed roses Jeffrey handed her when she opened the door Friday evening.

"Not half as beautiful as you, sweetheart," Jeffrey growled in a fairly good imitation of Humphrey Bogart.

Elizabeth giggled. "Come on in a minute. I want to put these in water right away."

Jeffrey followed her down the hall to the kitchen. "That's not the last surprise of the evening, either," he promised.

Elizabeth turned to face him. Jeffrey had asked her to go out to dinner and had told her to wear a dress, but he hadn't said anything about where they would be going for dinner. "Where are you taking me?" she asked, her eyes sparkling.

"I was thinking maybe pizza," he teased.

Elizabeth punched him playfully on the arm. "I didn't wear *silk* to eat *pepperoni!*"

Jeffrey glanced at her appreciatively. "Don't worry," he said, his voice low and warm. "I wouldn't waste all that on Guido's Pizza Palace!"

Elizabeth laughed. Then she turned and found a vase in a kitchen cabinet. After filling it with water, she arranged the roses, then put her face close and breathed in deeply. "These smell wonderful!" she exclaimed. "Thank you *so* much, Jeffrey."

Jeffrey bent forward, and his lips brushed hers in a quick kiss. "You're welcome," he said. He took her hand. "Let's go. I don't want to be late." Hand in hand, they walked to his car.

As he backed the car out of the Wakefield driveway, Jeffrey felt relaxed and happy—for the first time since Elizabeth had told him her former boyfriend was moving back to town. Elizabeth seemed to be feeling the same way, he thought. *If only we could always be like this. Alone, just the two of us, driving away from Sweet Valley and everyone who lives here!*

But Jeffrey knew that a relationship could never exist in a vacuum. If he and Elizabeth were to remain together as a couple, then they both had to come to terms with Todd Wilkins.

He headed north along the Valley Crest Highway. The breeze flowing through the car's open windows smelled of pine.

"*I* know where we're going!" Elizabeth exclaimed just as Jeffrey flicked on his turn signal. "The Valley Inn!"

"You guessed correctly, Miss Wakefield! You win a romantic dinner for two at the Valley Inn with the man of your choice—providing that's me!"

Jeffrey parked the car in front of the charming old restaurant nestled in a grove of Douglas firs overlooking the ocean. An attendant took the keys, and Jeffrey offered his arm to Elizabeth. "Was this an OK choice?" he asked.

"OK?" She squeezed his arm. "You bet it is! But, Jeffrey, we didn't have to come someplace this fancy."

"I know, but I wanted to make this a special Friday night," he explained. "It's been a while since we did something out of the ordinary, just the two of us."

"You're right." Elizabeth reached up to straighten Jeffrey's tie as they waited for the hostess to take them to their reserved table. "I'm glad you had this idea! This old inn is magical."

That's what I'm hoping, thought Jeffrey as they followed the hostess to the back of the restaurant to a cozy table for two with a view of the water. He felt he was going to need all the help he could get to hold on to Elizabeth's love. A little magic couldn't hurt.

Facing Elizabeth across the table, the last rays of the sunset sparkling like diamonds in her blond hair, it was easy for Jeffrey to almost forget the torture he'd gone through the past week. *Almost.* Elizabeth couldn't hide the effect Todd's return was having on her, and she hadn't

44

denied she was still attracted to her old boyfriend. Of course, it went without saying that Todd would still want to date Elizabeth. How could anyone not love Elizabeth Wakefield?

I can't lose you. Jeffrey dropped his eyes, pretending to study the menu. *I won't lose you. I won't just step aside and watch you go.*

He hadn't realized until this moment just how deeply he had come to care for Elizabeth. Jeffrey raised his glass of water, a half-smile creasing his face. "Hey, Liz, how about a toast? To tonight. To you and me."

Elizabeth echoed Jeffrey's toast. "To us," she said, taking a sip of her water. "To tonight!"

After leaving the Valley Inn, Jeffrey drove north again on the oceanside highway. Now they were parked at the scenic overlook at Las Palmas Canyon. Far below, at the base of the breathtaking sheer cliffs, Whitewater River raced through the gorge to the sea.

After a few moments spent silently admiring the view, washed in soft silver light by the full moon above, Jeffrey tipped Elizabeth's face to his.

The kiss was long and tender, and Elizabeth thought she might melt in Jeffrey's arms. The moment was like a beautiful dream, one she wished would never end.

With a quiet sigh, Elizabeth pulled away and rested her head against Jeffrey's shoulder.

"That was nice," he murmured into her hair.

"Umm-hmm," she agreed.

"I wouldn't mind sitting here for the rest of our lives."

"I know what you mean." The dreamlike spot had obviously cast its spell on them both. But dreams didn't last forever, even if one wanted them to. Elizabeth had learned that the hard way when Todd moved to Vermont.

"Jeffrey—"

"Don't say it, Liz," he interrupted. "I know what you're thinking. This place isn't the real world, and we'd go nuts if we tried to sit here for the rest of our lives!"

Elizabeth laughed. "Something like that."

"What I really meant was"—his arm tightened around her shoulders—"being with you, that's what I want to last. These past few months . . ." Jeffrey's words trailed off, and when he spoke again his voice was husky. "These past few months with you have been the best, happiest times of my life."

"Oh, Jeffrey." Her own voice trembled with emotion.

"Do you feel the same way, Liz? That we belong together?"

Jeffrey's question pierced right to the core of the conflict that was splitting Elizabeth's heart in two. *Did* she and Jeffrey belong together? Right now, at this instant, it seemed they did. "You're such a special, wonderful person," Elizabeth said, placing her hands on either side of his face. "I care about you so much."

Jeffrey stared into Elizabeth's eyes. "Does that mean yes?"

"Oh, Jeffrey," she whispered, her heart aching. "I *think* it does, but—I'm still not sure." The disappointment that shadowed Jeffrey's face was unmistakable, but she couldn't encourage him to hope until she honestly *could* swear they belonged together. And right now her feelings for Todd made that impossible.

"When I've worked things out, when I know for sure what part I want Todd to play in my life . . . Jeffrey, you'll be the first to know," Elizabeth promised, putting her lips to his to kiss the hurt away.

"I'm banking on Todd," Ken Matthews declared.

"Not me. I think it'll be Jeffrey," Aaron Dallas predicted with conviction.

"You guys are terrible! Why don't you just start a betting pool?" Jessica pretended to be appalled, but secretly she was as anxious as anyone to find out who her twin would choose. She knew it was difficult for Elizabeth, but her twin was in a position most girls would envy— she had her choice of two gorgeous guys! It was just like the plot of a soap opera. For once Jessica had to admit that Elizabeth's life was racier than her own.

But as far as wagering which boy would win Elizabeth's love, at this point it looked like a draw to Jessica. When Elizabeth and Jeffrey had arrived at Winston's party half an hour earlier, they seemed like a pair very much in love. Jessica knew Jeffrey had splurged on a romantic dinner at the Valley Inn the night before. Then he and Elizabeth spent all of Saturday together, finishing up with a picnic at the beach before swinging by Winston's.

But Todd was at the party, too—in fact, he was the guest of honor. And from the moment Elizabeth spotted Todd, she appeared to be in agony.

Jessica searched the room for her sister again. She spotted Elizabeth and Jeffrey standing with Enid and her boyfriend, Hugh Grayson, and a couple of other friends. Jeffrey had one arm possessively around Elizabeth's waist.

Enjoy it while you can, Jeffrey, thought Jessica, eyeing Todd speculatively. *Of course Liz is too nice to dump you outright. But once she's realized how much more Todd has to offer her, I'm afraid you'll be history!*

"Excuse me, you two." Jessica walked away from Aaron and Ken, flashing them both a big smile. They were both very attractive—she had dated each of them a number of times. In fact, not too long ago she had contemplated falling in love with Ken for lack of anything better to do. The romantic possibilities at Sweet Valley High were really wearing thin! she thought. But now a whole new world was about to open up before her, Jessica was convinced. She was going to have access to a whole new student body—or bodies, she thought, giggling.

When Elizabeth resumed her romance with Todd, Jessica was going to meet lots of good-looking, rich guys at Lovett Academy. She was sure of it. She just had to get Todd and Elizabeth together—and soon!

Jessica strolled up to Todd, who was talking with Amy Sutton and Bruce Patman. "Todd, how *are* you!" she said cheerfully.

"Hey, Jess." Todd slung an arm around her shoulders. "What's up?"

"Absolutely nothing!" Jessica exclaimed. "What are *you* three up to? I bet Todd's telling stories about his new school. Am I right?"

"No, actually, we were talking about—" Bruce began.

Jessica cut him off. "So, how *is* Lovett, Todd? By now you must know a whole bunch of interesting people. . . ."

A few minutes later Bruce and Amy drifted off to dance. As soon as Jessica had Todd to herself, she pumped him for information about Lovett.

After answering a few questions, Todd seemed sick of the subject. "Jessica, what can I do to get you to quit bugging me about Lovett? I'll promise you anything," he said.

Jessica grinned. She had him exactly where she wanted him. "Well, since you *asked*. . . . How about taking Liz and me up to Lovett with you one day next week? We'd love a tour of the campus and a chance to meet some of your new friends."

At the mention of Elizabeth's name, a hopeful expression brightened Todd's face. "I'd love to show you two around," he agreed eagerly. "You think Liz really wants to go?"

"She's dying to see the academy," Jessica fibbed. As a matter of fact, she couldn't remember Elizabeth saying anything at all about Lovett. If anything, Jessica had the feeling Elizabeth was uneasy about Todd's new school. But Jessica was certain Elizabeth would come around once she saw Todd in his new environment. *Lovett Academy, here I come!* Jessica thought triumphantly.

But first she wanted to take advantage of the situation. Both Jeffrey and Todd were at the party. If they were standing side by side, it would be so much easier for Elizabeth to make her decision—and Jessica had no doubt that her sister would choose Todd once she saw the obvious advantages he had.

"Um, Todd," Jessica said, "you haven't met Jeffrey yet, have you? I know you might feel a little funny about it," she hurried to add, "but that's all the more reason to get it over with."

"You're probably right," Todd admitted, his voice flat.

"I know I'm right," Jessica pressed. "And I know Liz'll feel a lot better about—things once she's seen you and Jeffrey shake hands."

Todd straightened his shoulders. "Then let's do it."

Making their way through the crowd, he and Jessica approached Elizabeth, Jeffrey, and the others.

Conversation stopped abruptly when the group caught sight of Jessica and Todd. Before stepping into the silence, Jessica had time to notice that while Todd remained composed, Jeffrey looked extremely nervous. *That's natural*, she thought. *He has a lot more to lose.*

Elizabeth, meanwhile, went pale. Jessica could see her twin wasn't going to be of much help. "Todd, you remember all these characters, don't you?" Jessica asked, smiling. "Oh, that's right. Jeffrey's new to town since you moved. Jeffrey French, meet Todd Wilkins."

As he extended his right hand, Jeffrey resembled a department store mannequin. "Heard a lot about you, Todd. Welcome back," he practically croaked.

Todd was equally stiff. "Thanks. Nice to meet you," he responded.

Jessica smiled with secret satisfaction as Enid, attempting to dispel the awkwardness of the moment, began chattering.

Elizabeth stared at the floor in embarrassment, so Jessica couldn't catch her eye. She sent a silent message to her twin instead. *Take a good look, Liz. Here they are, side by side. Isn't it obvious which one is Mr. Right?*

Six

"That's Wolfe Hall, one of the dorms." Todd pointed to an elegant Spanish-style building. "Where the party is," he added.

"So not everybody at Lovett's a day student like you?" Jessica asked.

"Nope. It's about fifty-fifty. Half boarders and half commuters," Todd explained.

Jessica nodded, filing this fact away along with the others she had absorbed so far that afternoon. Elizabeth remained quiet. As the three neared Wolfe Hall and the party, Jessica's animation and Elizabeth's apprehension both increased. *Why can't I relax and enjoy this like Jessica?* Elizabeth asked herself.

It was Thursday afternoon, the week after Winston's party. Todd had called the night before to propose the visit. He was really going out of his way—making two round trips from

Sweet Valley to Cedar Springs in one day just so Elizabeth and Jessica could see his new school. Elizabeth appreciated the gesture. Todd wanted to include her in his new life, and that made her happy.

But the minute they drove through the gates of Lovett, Elizabeth began to feel intimidated. The grounds and buildings of the school were so *lush*. And the students!

These weren't Sweet Valley kids in T-shirts and jeans. A lot of the guys wore jackets and ties, and the girls wore the latest styles. Elizabeth felt distinctly unglamorous in her simple cotton jersey dress. The whole place made her feel as if she were trespassing at an exclusive country club.

Country clubs . . . that reminded Elizabeth of the latest rumor that was being passed around Sweet Valley High by Lila Fowler. Todd's family now belonged to the country club. Lila, also a member, claimed Todd was frequenting the tennis courts with the daughter of the chairman of Varitronics, a friend of Lila's. Elizabeth tried to remember her name. Was it Cathy Kane . . . or Candy Kane? She grinned.

She didn't exactly trust Lila to speak the truth, so for the moment Elizabeth was inclined to ignore this latest piece of gossip. She had enough to worry about as it was. Even though she had been spending time with both Jeffrey and Todd, she wasn't any closer to determining which of them held first place in her heart. If anything, as the days passed she found herself caring more for each of them.

As Todd proudly showed Elizabeth and Jessica around Lovett's classrooms, library, sports complex, and athletic fields, he tried to draw Elizabeth into the conversation. She did her best to appear interested—she *was* interested. But the more she saw, the more she wished Todd was back at Sweet Valley High with her.

When they entered the lobby of Wolfe Hall, Todd was immediately accosted by an exotic-looking girl with straight black hair in a Cleopatra-style cut. "Todd! Glad you could make it!" the girl exclaimed.

Todd greeted her with an easygoing smile. "Wouldn't have missed it," he assured her. "Any excuse to get out of the library for a few hours!"

"Well, get on in there." The girl, who hadn't so much as glanced at Elizabeth and Jessica, gave Todd a flirtatious smile. "People have been looking for you."

What sort of people? Elizabeth wondered.

They found the party in the large common room at the end of the hallway. Elizabeth caught her breath. Tall French doors opened out into a palm-filled courtyard. Overhead, crystal chandeliers glimmered. Beneath their feet was a genuine Persian carpet.

This could be Fowler Crest or the Patman mansion! Elizabeth thought, awed. She couldn't believe this was a dorm.

"Todd, I see you brought Elizabeth," a deep

male voice observed. Then the speaker chuckled. "Whoa—*two* Elizabeths!"

Jessica and Elizabeth both turned and looked right into the clear blue eyes of a boy who could have passed for a young Paul Newman. Elizabeth felt Jessica elbow her sharply in the ribs.

"Yep, this is Elizabeth Wakefield—Liz." Todd put an arm around her waist, and Elizabeth suddenly felt relaxed and secure. It was reassuring to know Todd had told at least one of his new friends about her. "And this is Jessica, Liz's twin sister. Liz, Jess, I'd like you to meet Sheffield Eastman."

Sheffield shook their hands, dazzling them with a perfect smile. But despite his looks and the designer cut of his sports jacket, his manner wasn't in the least snobby. "I'm glad to meet you both," he said.

"It's nice to meet you," Elizabeth responded.

Jessica flashed him her most dazzling smile. "It's *very* nice to meet you!" she said.

Maybe this is going to be all right, Elizabeth thought, her spirits lifting.

"Why, hello, Todd!"

The girl now facing Elizabeth made the pretty girl in the lobby look dull as dishwater. She was tall, and a body-hugging suede dress made the most of her curves. Rich mahogany-brown hair, parted on the side, fell in a sleek curtain against one bronzed cheek. Clusters of wine-red rubies sparkled at her ears.

"Courtney! Hi. Um, I'd like you to meet two

friends of mine from Sweet Valley High—Elizabeth and Jessica Wakefield.'' To the twins he said, "This is Courtney Kane."

Courtney Kane! All of a sudden Elizabeth wished she had paid more attention to Lila's country club story. Todd had been playing tennis with *this* girl? "Hello, Courtney," she managed to get out. Jessica was so wrapped up in talking to Sheffield that she didn't even notice Courtney's arrival.

Courtney ran her smoky eyes up and down Elizabeth without saying anything. Then she turned her attention back to Todd. "I wanted to thank you again for the *wonderful* time last night! The reception would have been unbearably dull without you. But I *really* enjoyed myself."

Elizabeth didn't fail to pick up on Todd's embarrassment. "Oh, yeah. I had fun, too, Courtney," he said quickly.

"Let's do it again sometime, shall we?" Courtney said in her sultry, assured tone. "I can see you're busy, but I'm *sure* I'll catch you later. So long, Todd."

"Bye, Courtney."

Elizabeth watched the other girl stroll away. "She seems . . . nice," she said, straining to sound nonchalant.

Todd shrugged. "She's nice enough. What she was talking about—last night—"

Elizabeth quickly interrupted Todd. "You don't have to explain anything to me."

"Maybe not, but I want to." They were alone

now, Jessica having moved off a few feet to talk with Sheffield. "Liz, it wasn't like a date or anything. There was this reception for Varitronics VIP types and their families. Courtney's dad is, well, he's the chairman of the board for Varitronics."

"So you and Courtney just happened to be at the same reception," Elizabeth said.

"Well, not exactly." Todd shifted his feet, frowning. "I kind of escorted her. Now that my dad's president of Varitronics, well, there are certain social obligations he has to fulfill—*we* have to fulfill as a family."

Elizabeth paled slightly. "So what you're saying is that you *had* to be Courtney's date because of your dad's new position. Kind of like having to attend private school?" *And playing tennis at the club?* she added silently.

"Exactly." Todd appeared relieved that Elizabeth understood. "It's all pretty dull, Liz. This school, and that reception last night. Believe me, I'd much rather be hanging out at the Dairi Burger."

As they made their way to the refreshment table for a drink, Elizabeth wished she could believe Todd. But it didn't look dull to Elizabeth. Todd seemed to be enjoying himself.

Which was fine, Elizabeth decided firmly. She was dating another boy and had absolutely no claim on Todd. He was free to date dozens of girls if he liked. And, really, he must think she was naive if he expected her to believe that escorting rich, beautiful Courtney Kane was a *chore* to him.

Why doesn't Todd just come right out and say it? Elizabeth thought, accepting a glass of iced tea garnished with lemon. He had only invited her to Lovett today because he felt it was the polite thing to do. But taking her and Jessica for a tour and letting them tag along at this party—that was the *real* chore.

I might as well face it, Elizabeth told herself. *Todd belongs to an exclusive social circle now—and I don't. Things will never be the same between us again.*

"*Africa?* Wow. I would *love* to go there!" Jessica exclaimed. "You went on a real safari and everything?"

Sheffield smiled at her enthusiasm. "Well, I guess you could call it that. But I assure you we traveled comfortably, with all the amenities. My mother's not the sort to rough it!"

"I can relate." Jessica nodded. "You wouldn't catch *me* prowling around in the bush without my blow dryer!"

He laughed, and the deep, hearty sound thrilled Jessica all the way to her toes. *Sheffield Eastman*, she said to herself, admiring him over the rim of her glass, *where have you been all my life? Thank you, Todd Wilkins!* she thought, throwing Todd a grateful glance.

"So, Jessica. You're from Sweet Valley like

Todd?" When she nodded, Sheffield added, "That's a beautiful town. Courtney Kane lives there, too."

Jessica stifled a scowl. She hadn't paid much attention to Courtney, but it only took one glance to see that she was outrageously snobbish. The way she had drooled over Todd was disgusting. "Is that so?" she remarked sweetly.

"She and Todd belong to the same country club, I believe."

Jessica didn't like the sound of that, but she was more interested in learning about Sheffield than Courtney. "How about you, Sheffield? Where are you from? Do you board at Lovett?"

"My family lives right here in Cedar Springs," he informed her. "I could practically walk to school." His blue eyes twinkled. "But I'm too lazy. I confess—I drive!"

Jessica fought back an urge to ask *what* he drove—a Mercedes or a Porsche. "I just love this area," she said.

"Me, too. I guess my family's always had a thing for Cedar Springs. Eastmans have been living here for nearly a hundred years!"

"How wonderful!" Jessica sighed. She could imagine the history: Sheffield's great-great-grandfather carving an empire out of the western wilderness. Sheffield's family probably *founded* Cedar Springs. He was just too modest to say so! "I suppose you've been at Lovett for a while, then."

"Yep. I've never gone to any other school.

It's a great place, but sometimes I wish I'd had the chance to see what public school was like. It's a privilege to attend Lovett, but it's not exactly the real world."

Jessica liked Sheffield more than ever. Obviously he was only saying that so she wouldn't think he looked down on her for going to a public high school. What a gentleman. "Don't worry. You're not missing anything," she assured him. "You're lucky!"

"I *am* lucky," agreed Sheffield, his expression thoughtful. "In fact, that's why I'm going to take some time off from school. I'm planning an independent project that'll give me a chance to really explore one of my more serious interests—" Sheffield stopped, his attention diverted. "Jessica, Todd's signaling to us. It looks like he's ready to go."

Drat, Jessica thought. *Just when Sheffield's telling me his most private plans and dreams!* She recalled the African safari story. His independent project was bound to be something equally glamorous, probably with an international angle. He looked like a yachtsman. Maybe he was going to sail solo around the world. Maybe he'd inherited a castle in England or a vineyard in France and had to go abroad to check it out.

Elizabeth and Todd were halfway out the door, but Jessica didn't intend to leave the party disappointed. She had to think up a way to see Sheffield again. But before she could say anything, Sheffield spoke up.

"Jessica, I really enjoyed talking with you," he said earnestly. "I'd like to call you, if you don't mind."

Mind? Are you crazy? "I hope you will," Jessica encouraged him, trying to sound nonchalant. "Todd knows my number."

Jessica floated out of Wolfe Hall fantasizing about future double dates. Elizabeth and Todd . . . and her and Sheffield.

"Thanks for the tour, Todd, it was fantastic, see ya!" Jessica said all in one breath as she leapt out of the BMW.

Elizabeth shook her head. "That's my sister," she observed wryly. "Always so subtle!"

"I don't mind!" Todd turned the key in the ignition, killing the engine. "She thought we might like some privacy, and she was right."

Elizabeth looked down at her hands, folded in her lap. "Well, here we are."

There was a moment of silence. Outside the car the chirping of crickets brought music to the Southern California night. Todd cleared his throat. "Thanks, Liz, for coming out with me to Lovett today," he began. "It made the place seem warmer, somehow. Even just having you there for a few hours."

Elizabeth met his eyes. She wanted to believe he meant that. But what about Courtney Kane?

Todd seemed to pick up on her uncertainty. "I know this is still a little awkward. It's going to be awhile before I get used to all the changes at home myself. But, Liz, I haven't changed."

Elizabeth smiled, her heart warmed by a sudden surge of tenderness. "Still the same old Todd?" she teased.

"You bet." Todd's eyes crinkled. "You can't teach an old dog new tricks. Speaking of old tricks, I'm thinking of having a party in a week or so. It'll be a chance to get old friends and new friends together, welcome everybody to my folks' new house."

Elizabeth nodded. "That's a great idea," she said.

"I hope you'll come." Todd paused. "You will come, won't you?" he repeated.

"Of course! And now I should be getting inside." Elizabeth put a hand on the door. Before opening it, she turned to face Todd to say goodbye.

Without speaking, he bent toward her. Instinctively Elizabeth lifted her face. Todd's lips brushed hers tentatively. For a sudden, startling fraction of a second, it seemed that their mouths might meet in a real kiss.

Then Elizabeth pulled back. What was she doing? Todd wasn't her boyfriend! "Bye!" she said, stepping rapidly from the car to mask her confusion.

Todd beeped the BMW's horn in farewell as he pulled out of the Wakefields' driveway. Elizabeth waved and then turned toward the house.

She could still feel the momentary warmth of Todd's lips on her own. And that wasn't all she felt. A number of emotions were struggling inside her.

Todd had wanted to kiss her. Maybe that proved Courtney Kane didn't mean anything to him. The thought made Elizabeth feel good. But at the same time she was overwhelmed with guilt. She and Todd hadn't really kissed, but she had wanted to as much as he had. Jeffrey would be so hurt if he knew how strong her feelings for Todd had become.

Inside, Elizabeth found her mother sitting at the kitchen table, flipping through photographs of a house she had decorated.

"Hi, Mom!" she said as cheerfully as she could.

"Hi, honey. Jeffrey phoned about half an hour ago." Alice Wakefield looked up at Elizabeth with a welcoming smile. "I told him you'd call back when you got in."

Elizabeth couldn't help it. She burst into tears and ran out of the room.

Jessica caught Elizabeth's arm as she dashed past her on the stairs. "Liz, what's the matter?" she demanded, obviously shocked by the intensity of her twin's sobs.

Without answering, Elizabeth ran into her bedroom. Jessica followed. "Liz, talk to me! Tell me what's wrong. Maybe I can help."

"Oh, Jess!" Elizabeth flung her arms around her sister, still crying so hard she could barely get the words out.

Jessica patted Elizabeth's back. "Hey, it'll be OK," she said soothingly.

"No, it won't," Elizabeth moaned. She pushed Jessica away and reached for the box of tissues next to her bed.

"Elizabeth, what happened? Five minutes ago I left you in the car with Todd, and you were fine!"

Elizabeth sank onto the edge of her bed, dabbing her eyes with a tissue. "I was only fine on the surface. Inside I'm so confused!"

"Of course you're confused," Jessica said. "Anybody would be."

"It's just that I don't see any way out." Elizabeth shook her head.

"There's a way out of every situation," Jessica reminded Elizabeth. "Things are never as rotten as they seem."

"Wanna bet?" Elizabeth blew her nose. "Jess, no matter what I do, somebody will end up getting hurt. Jeffrey or Todd—or me."

"Just take care of yourself, Liz," Jessica advised gently, touching Elizabeth's arm. "You're the one whose feelings matter most."

Elizabeth smiled at her through a mist of tears. "Thanks, Jess," she whispered. "I'll try."

Seven

"Do you want to talk about it, sweetheart?"

It was Saturday morning, and Elizabeth and her mother were sitting alone at the breakfast table. Mr. Wakefield was already out in the yard mowing the lawn, and Jessica, a dedicated late sleeper, wasn't expected out of bed for hours.

"It has to do with Todd and Jeffrey, doesn't it?" Mrs. Wakefield probed delicately.

Elizabeth smiled. "How did you guess?"

Mrs. Wakefield laughed. "Oh, it's just a little trick we mothers have. It's called putting two and two together."

"I just don't know what to do," Elizabeth confessed quietly. "I care so much about Jeffrey. We've had so many wonderful times together. I can't imagine not sharing my life with him. But at the same time, when I saw Todd again, I realized that deep inside I'd never stopped loving him. It's like being torn right down the middle, Mom."

Reaching across the table, Mrs. Wakefield squeezed her daughter's hand. "I know you've been under a strain, honey. There are no easy answers to questions like this."

"I have to come up with one, though!" Elizabeth said vehemently. "I can't sleep, I can't concentrate on my homework. I spend all my time making mental lists, comparing my relationships with Todd and Jeffrey, trying to figure out who I like more!"

Mrs. Wakefield frowned thoughtfully and tapped a neatly filed fingernail against her teacup. "Liz, when you first met Todd, did you make a mental list of his good and bad points so you could decide whether or not he should become your boyfriend?"

Elizabeth giggled despite her unhappiness. "Of course not! We just fell in love."

"And what about Jeffrey? When you were getting to know him, did you rate his personality and looks on a scale of one to ten?"

Elizabeth began to see what her mother was getting at. "No," she admitted.

Mrs. Wakefield smiled gently. "Then that approach isn't going to work now. Honey, the confusion will pass. You just have to be patient with yourself. It's going to take time."

"It's hard to be patient," Elizabeth observed with a shaky sigh. "I can't help thinking about it!"

"Maybe you should try *thinking* a little less," her mother suggested, "and feeling a little more. You need to listen to your heart."

For a few minutes Elizabeth and her mother sat without speaking. The far-off buzzing noise of the lawn mower and the sweet scent of fresh-cut grass drifted through the window.

Gradually a feeling of peace settled over Elizabeth. It was true. She would never get anywhere comparing Todd and Jeffrey in a mathematical way. A relationship couldn't be reduced to an equation.

There was still something bothering her, though. She told her mother about Courtney Kane and how rumors had been circulating about how much time Todd and Courtney were spending together. "So what if I listen to my heart and it tells me I care more for Todd, but meanwhile Todd's listening to *his* heart and it tells him *he* likes Courtney?" Elizabeth asked.

"There's always that possibility. But I think you're blowing this Courtney thing out of proportion," Mrs. Wakefield said. "It's natural for Todd to have new friends, both because of his father's new job and Todd's new school. But as far as Courtney is concerned, I'd take Todd's word on the subject before Lila's any day."

Elizabeth smiled gratefully. "Mom, how come you're so smart?" she asked, scooting around the table to give her mother a hug.

* * *

Elizabeth was trying to listen to her heart, but with Jessica, Lila, and Cara Walker gabbing so loudly it was impossible!

The morning had blossomed into a flawless Southern California afternoon, and the twins were lounging by their pool with a few friends. Elizabeth and Enid, off to one side, were doing some homework while they tanned. Jessica, Cara, and Lila, on the other hand, had just returned from an exhausting trip to the Valley Mall, and they couldn't stop talking about it.

"I should have bought those raw silk trousers at Bibi's," Jessica lamented, rolling over on her towel.

"Told you so!" Lila sang as she smoothed suntan lotion on her golden-brown arms.

"But they were so expensive," Jessica continued. "Mom and Dad would've killed me if I'd charged them."

"Don't forget, the sale at Lisette's starts next weekend," Cara reminded her. "You'll probably find just as nice a pair for a lot less. Bibi's stuff is overpriced anyway."

"Maybe you're right." Jessica frowned. "Still, they were the softest raw silk. They draped so nicely. And the *color* matched my eyes perfectly!" she wailed.

"Jessica, why don't you just go back to the mall and *buy* the pants and spare us your moaning and groaning?" Elizabeth burst out, slamming shut her American history textbook.

Jessica sat up on her towel and stared at her sister. It wasn't like Elizabeth to snap. "Well, excu-u-u-se me. What's the matter with you?"

"Oh, nothing." Elizabeth sighed heavily as she adjusted the back of her chaise longue. Tipping her face to the sun, she closed her eyes. "Sorry, Jess."

"That's OK, Liz," she said, flopping back onto her towel. "Maybe I *will* go back to Bibi's later. The pants should still be there. They had two size sixes. And there's a matching top . . ."

Elizabeth had to laugh. For a minute she wished she could trade places with Jessica. The biggest dilemma in her twin's life was how to scheme enough money out of their parents to buy a new outfit.

Just relax, Elizabeth told herself, allowing the warmth of the sun to dissolve the tension in her body.

"I'd go back and get the pants if I were you," Lila recommended. "With the top, it might be just the thing to wear to Todd's party."

"Todd's party?" repeated Jessica, darting a look at her twin. Elizabeth herself was surprised at Lila's remark. Todd had mentioned on Thursday that he was planning a party, but it hadn't sounded like a big deal. How would Lila have heard about it?

"That's what I said." Lila gazed speculatively at Elizabeth. "You know all about it, don't you, Liz?"

"Well, Todd *did* mention something about a party," Elizabeth responded nonchalantly.

Lila folded her arms underneath her head. "Once the invitations are out, it's going to be all anybody talks about," she predicted.

"Invitations? You mean this is a *formal* party?" Jessica asked.

"Formal? It's probably going to be the biggest, splashiest event Sweet Valley's seen in ages! At least since *my* last party," Lila amended.

"Wow." Jessica whistled. "That doesn't sound like Todd's style to me. He was always such a casual kind of guy, right, Liz?"

"Hmm," murmured Elizabeth. She didn't want to admit she wasn't sure what Todd's style was anymore.

"Well, it's Todd's style *now*," Lila said archly. "It's going to be sort of a housewarming party, to reestablish himself in Sweet Valley. Now that his father's president of Varitronics, well, that makes Todd a pretty important person, too."

Elizabeth frowned. A housewarming party to reestablish himself in Sweet Valley? That didn't sound like Todd. It sounded like another social obligation, something Todd was expected to do as the son of the company president.

There was one question bothering Elizabeth. Fortunately, Jessica spared her the necessity of asking it. "Li, how do *you* know all the dirt on Todd's party?" Jessica demanded.

Lila readjusted her towel to the changing angle of the sun. "Well, I have a friend at the country club. Her name's Courtney Kane, and she's *fabulously* interesting."

Courtney Kane? Elizabeth gripped the arms of her lounge chair more tightly.

"Yeah," Jessica said in a bored voice. "We met her the other day at Lovett with Todd. But I don't know about 'fabulously interesting,' Lila. She struck me as a super-snob airhead. Didn't she, Lizzie?"

Elizabeth giggled, but Lila was not amused. "Oh, Jessica," she said, "don't be so gauche! I'm sure if you had a chance to spend more time with Courtney, you'd like her as much as I do."

Jessica's sour expression contradicted this, but Lila continued, oblivious. "Anyway, Courtney told me about it yesterday. She'd just finished a tennis game with Todd, and she was bursting with the news!"

Elizabeth felt nauseated. Another tennis game at the club with Courtney Kane? Todd's idea of a good time used to be shooting baskets with the guys. Since when was he so into tennis? Since he became an "important" person?

A terrible doubt began to take shape in Elizabeth's mind. If what Lila said was true, Todd's party wasn't going to be the informal gathering of friends she had imagined. It sounded more like some kind of formal ball!

How would she fit into Todd's plans? He had

mentioned the party to her, so obviously he wanted her to be there. But in what role? Would he be calling to ask her *formally* to be his date at his *formal* party? Would this be the occasion to let the whole valley know his heart still belonged to her? The thought made Elizabeth's pulse race with hopeful anticipation.

But what if Todd got stuck escorting Courtney again? It was possible there would be pressure from his family to invite Courtney to the party as his date just because Mr. Kane was chairman of the board.

Elizabeth didn't have to fret over this question for long. Lila still had some information up her sleeve, and obviously she had saved the choicest tidbit for last. "Yes, Courtney told me *all*," Lila continued meaningfully. "The party will be catered, and there'll be a live band. And Todd asked her to be his date at the party. Actually, not only his date—she's going to act as cohost!"

Todd and Courtney. Can it really be true? Elizabeth took a deep breath to calm herself while Enid quickly steered the conversation to another topic. If she had heard the story from anyone else but Lila, Elizabeth would have been convinced of its truth. But Lila Fowler was famous for saying anything that enabled her to create a sensation. So it was possible that Lila's scoop on the party, including the bit about Courtney acting as cohost, was an exaggeration. If so, it wouldn't be the first rumor Lila had passed along.

Swallowing her doubt and pain, Elizabeth re-opened her history book. She had to keep an open mind. Next time she spoke with Todd, she was sure she would hear the real story.

Eight

"I think I'll ride Moonshadow today, Cliff," Courtney said, tapping her leather crop idly against her leg.

"That's fine," remarked the head groom at the Lovett Academy stables. "Shadow's already saddled up and ready to go. Just make sure you have him back in about an hour. We need him for a lesson."

"I'll see what I can do," Courtney teased in an airy, unconcerned tone.

Placing one booted foot in the stirrup, Courtney swung herself up onto the back of the dark chestnut horse. She didn't mind the look of admiration in Cliff's eyes. He was kind of cute, even if he *was* just a groom. And Courtney knew she deserved the admiration. She was very aware that her close-fitting riding breeches and crisply tailored white shirt were flattering.

She and Moonshadow started off at a trot, Courtney saluting Cliff with the crop. "Ta-ta!"

"An hour, Courtney!" he called after her.

An hour would be plenty of time, but Courtney liked to keep Cliff guessing. Without a backward glance, she guided Moonshadow toward the bridle path and urged him into a gentle canter.

It was a beautiful, sunny Monday. *And everything's going my way!* Courtney thought, smiling. She recalled her conversation with Lila Fowler at the country club on Friday. Lila had been shameless. She might as well have taken notes. But after all, that was what Courtney wanted. She *wanted* Lila to absorb every word and then repeat them syllable for syllable for Elizabeth Wakefield's benefit.

"Poor Lila," Courtney said out loud to Moonshadow, ducking her head to avoid a low tree branch. "It really is too bad her father didn't send her to Lovett. She has everything in the world going for her, but she could use a little *polish*."

In the past Courtney hadn't had much use for Lila, even though she knew Lila wanted to be friends with her; it was blatantly obvious that the girl wanted to wangle her way into the exclusive Lovett crowd. Then Courtney learned Lila was best friends with Elizabeth Wakefield's twin sister, Jessica. And Elizabeth Wakefield was the only obstacle between Courtney and what she wanted most in the world, for the moment at least—Todd Wilkins.

As Moonshadow cantered easily along, Courtney daydreamed about Todd. Tall, dark, and handsome—amusing, intelligent, and rich—he had everything! Best of all, he was somebody *new*. And, really, with the Varitronics connection, it was obvious they were meant for each other. The son of the company president was definitely worthy of her companionship.

Todd liked her and found her attractive, Courtney felt sure. She had never met a guy who *didn't* like her. And she was equally sure Todd secretly wanted her to be his date at the big party he was planning. It was only natural. From all appearances, however, he still harbored an attachment to his old Sweet Valley girlfriend. Courtney hadn't been very impressed by her "rival" when she met her at the Wolfe Hall party. Elizabeth was pretty enough in a sweet, goody-two-shoes way. But obviously the relationship was just a quaint holdover from Todd's pre-Lovett days.

So it hadn't really been a lie. Todd *would* ask Courtney to be his date once he heard the news about that Elizabeth and that Jeffrey person. And Elizabeth probably *would* settle down with Jeffrey now that she had to face the fact that she couldn't compete for Todd with Courtney Kane.

The bridle path cut around a small pond dotted with lily pads. On the right ran the low stucco wall bordering the Eastman estate. Another few strides and Courtney had a clear view of the Eastman tennis courts. Just as she had hoped, there was Sheffield, playing a game with his cute younger brother, Kent.

"Shef, hi!" Courtney called. She waved the crop in greeting. Sheffield shaded his eyes against the sun and then, recognizing her, smiled and walked over to the path.

Relaxing in the saddle, Courtney admired Sheffield's looks. With that spectacular Paul Newman face and a tanned muscular body to match, he was a work of art. Back when she dated Sheffield briefly, Courtney had enjoyed being seen with him. They had made a gorgeous pair. *Too bad Shef turned so boring!* You couldn't talk to him for five minutes these days before he started harping on one of his philanthropic schemes. It was all a big yawn.

But Shef's going to come in handy, just as Lila did! she thought with satisfaction.

"Nice day for a ride!" Sheffield observed, leaning his elbows on top of the stucco wall.

Courtney dismounted and jumped up onto the wall. Moonshadow's reins trailed idly in her hands. "Nice day for a set of tennis," she countered.

"Yeah, but you know how I hate to work up a sweat," Sheffield said with a grin. "And Kent's just getting too good at this game. He makes me *run!*"

Courtney laughed. "You can't fool me, Sheffield. You *like* to work. You're a grind at heart."

"Shh!" Sheffield put a finger to his lips. "You want to blow my cover?"

Courtney giggled. "Well, if Kent's too rough on you, you should ask Todd Wilkins over to play," Courtney suggested casually. "He's a very promising beginner. We've had a number of entertaining games at the club."

"Good idea!" Sheffield said enthusiastically. "You know, Todd's a great guy. Solid, down to earth, a lot of fun. I'm really glad he came to Lovett."

"Me, too," Courtney agreed. "I like him a lot. That's why I hate to think that he's going to get hurt. . . ." She let her sentence trail off temptingly.

Sheffield went for the bait. "Hurt? What do you mean?"

"I was talking to a *very* good friend of the Wakefield family the other day," Courtney began. "It sounds like Elizabeth Wakefield, the girl Todd used to date, is pretty hot and heavy with some other guy, Jeffrey somebody."

Sheffield frowned. "Todd did mention she was seeing somebody else. But he seemed to think there was a chance he and Elizabeth would get back together."

"Well, from what I hear, he shouldn't count on it," Courtney declared. "Supposedly Elizabeth and Jeffrey are more lovesick than ever. Jeffrey even gave her a *ring* recently. Maybe not an engagement ring, but the next best thing!"

Sheffield whistled. "Wow. I'm pretty sure Todd doesn't know anything about that."

"I didn't think so." Courtney tried her best to sound sincere. "I'm just glad he's not still at Sweet Valley High, where this whole thing would be rubbed right in his face."

"Yeah. But at least that way he wouldn't get his hopes up." Sheffield shook his head. "You know, I think he was going to ask Elizabeth to his party. He's mentioned the party to you, hasn't he?"

"Yes," confirmed Courtney. "And I know how psyched he is for it. Gosh, I hope this stuff about Elizabeth and Jeffrey doesn't come as too big a shock. It could spoil the party for him!"

"Yeah, it sure could," Sheffield said.

Courtney watched his face carefully. *It worked!* she thought, hiding her feeling of triumph. Next time Sheffield saw Todd, he would find a tactful way of passing this tidbit along to his new buddy, she was sure of it. As a good samaritan, Sheffield would welcome the chance to spare his friend Todd any pain and embarrassment.

Moonshadow tugged on the reins, giving Courtney an excuse to hop down from the wall. "I should be getting on with my ride," she told Sheffield. "The horse has to be back at the barn in half an hour."

"What, he has an appointment?" Sheffield joked.

"Actually, he does!" Courtney mounted, but before heading off she leaned down to confide

79

a few final words to Sheffield. "Shef, all of this about Elizabeth—I'm not sure if it's public knowledge. . . ."

"Gotcha." Sheffield patted her knee. "I'll be discreet. See you at school, Court."

Pressing her heels into Moonshadow's sides, Courtney smiled. "Ta-ta!"

"I just thought you'd like to know," Sheffield concluded, jabbing at the crushed ice in his cup with a straw. "Sorry to be the bearer of bad news, pal."

The two boys were taking a Monday night study break at the snack bar adjacent to the Lovett library. Todd was unable to hide his dismay. Sheffield tactfully lowered his eyes and studied the front page of the Lovett Academy newspaper lying on the table.

Todd realized he was clenching his fist around a potato chip bag, crushing the chips inside. Relaxing his hand, he slumped back in his chair. "Well, thanks—I guess!" He laughed hoarsely. "It's nice not to be the last to know. I suppose I could have figured . . ."

Sheffield glanced up, his eyes understanding. Then he resumed reading the paper. Todd, lost in painful speculation, ate a few salty potato chip fragments.

Maybe I am the last to know, he thought. *Maybe I just haven't been seeing what's staring me right in the face.*

Todd knew he shouldn't be surprised. When he moved back to Sweet Valley, he knew that Elizabeth was involved with Jeffrey. And, after all, the last time they had seen each other, he had been interested in Suzanne Devlin.

But Elizabeth had always held a special place in Todd's heart and memories. He had never stopped caring for her. And, more than anything, Todd wanted to resume his relationship with Elizabeth. He had made that as clear to her as he could; he was just waiting for a signal from her.

Now it appeared that Elizabeth was giving him a signal, all right, but it wasn't the one he wanted.

A jumble of conflicting memories ran through Todd's mind. The glowing expression on Elizabeth's face when she and Jeffrey had arrived at Winston's party last weekend . . . Elizabeth's withdrawn attitude at Lovett and the fact that it was Jessica, not Liz, who was so interested in his new campus . . . then afterward, the electricity that had passed between Elizabeth and him, the near kiss . . .

Maybe I had that moment all wrong, Todd thought. *Maybe Elizabeth wasn't feeling what I was feeling. It must have been all my imagination—I probably thought she was attracted to me just because I wanted her to be.*

Three girls sat down at the next table, chattering loudly and obviously intending to attract Todd's and Sheffield's attention. They were all pretty, but they didn't have the simple, natural style Todd liked. They had too much makeup, too much jewelry, too much perfume—and too little substance.

And there was Elizabeth. He imagined her soft, gentle fragrant hair, the way she always smelled fresh and sweet. He could *talk* to Elizabeth. She was *real*. And she cared about so many things. Todd had always admired her unselfish energy and ambition.

He sighed deeply. Spending time with Elizabeth had convinced Todd that he loved her as much as he ever had. But now he had to acknowledge defeat. He had returned to Sweet Valley too late to win her back.

"Do you want to talk about it?" Sheffield asked casually, pushing the newspaper aside.

Todd shrugged. "Unfortunately, there doesn't seem to be much to talk about. She's made her choice, and all I can do is step aside."

"That's tough," his friend commiserated.

"Yeah, it is," agreed Todd.

"Are you still going to have the party?"

"Sure," Todd said, but without much enthusiasm. "I've already lined up a band and a caterer. The invitations are almost ready to be mailed. My parents really wanted me to throw an all-out bash. I might as well go through with it."

"I'm psyched to meet your Sweet Valley friends. It'll be great," Sheffield predicted.

Todd wasn't so sure. The party would have

all the right ingredients for success, but he had a feeling he wouldn't enjoy himself. He had hoped to share the evening with Elizabeth . . . which reminded him—he needed a date.

Courtney Kane was the obvious choice. Inviting her to the party would make both his father and her father happy. Courtney was beautiful and glamorous. Most guys would be thrilled to date her.

But Courtney wasn't Elizabeth. She didn't even come close.

Nine

"Guess who just called me!" Jessica asked Lila excitedly.

"Who?" Lila asked curiously.

"Sheffield Eastman!" Jessica cried. "The guy I met at Lovett Academy. The absolutely gorgeous, phenomenally rich one!"

"Oh." Lila sounded irritated. Even over the phone Jessica knew what was coming. Whenever Lila felt jealous, she pretended she couldn't care less.

But Jessica didn't intend to be deprived of her opportunity to gloat. "You probably want to know why he called and every word he said," she declared, not giving Lila a chance to say no. "Well, I'll tell you!"

"I'm dying to hear," Lila said, her voice full of sarcasm.

"Let's see. It's Tuesday, which is five days

since we met. I bet he waited this long so I wouldn't think he was pushy. At the same time he didn't wait *too* long because he didn't want me to forget his name and everything."

"Get to the point!" Lila yelled. "Did he ask you out or what?"

"I'm getting to that!" Jessica promised, fully enjoying her moment of triumph. "So then we talked for a couple of minutes about school and stuff. And *then*—drumroll, please—he wanted to know what I was doing tonight. He's driving all the way down from Cedar Springs just to take me out for dessert and coffee!"

"Can't he afford dinner?" Lila asked.

"Of course he can, you idiot. But he has some kind of long meeting at school this afternoon, so he can't make it here until eight o'clock. But he also said he didn't want the whole week to go by without seeing me."

"Well, enjoy your dessert," Lila said. "I hope it makes you fat."

Jessica laughed. "Actually, Lila, there's another reason I'm calling." She hoped Lila wasn't too jealous and crabby to do her a little favor. "I've been rummaging through my closet for an hour and I don't have anything to wear."

"Jessica, you have tons of clothes," Lila objected.

"I know, but nothing that's right for tonight," Jessica complained. "And then I thought of that little red Italian knit dress of yours . . ."

85

"Jessica, that dress is brand-new! I've only worn it once!" protested Lila.

"So it's wasted just hanging in your closet," Jessica argued. "Wouldn't you rather see it put to good use?"

"Such as?"

Jessica grinned. "Such as totally impressing Sheffield Eastman!"

Talk about traveling in style! Sailing along the palm-lined streets of Sweet Valley in a midnight blue Mercedes with Sheffield Eastman at the wheel, Jessica knew she could definitely get used to it.

"I was thinking about Venezia," Sheffield said, naming a chic Italian restaurant just outside Sweet Valley. "Courtney recommended it, actually."

Even the mention of snobby Courtney Kane couldn't spoil Jessica's mood. "It's a terrific place," she agreed, crossing her legs so Sheffield could admire them more easily. "Excellent cappuccino and wonderful desserts."

"Just what I had in mind," he said. "And a quiet atmosphere. Good for talking, I hope?"

"Uh-hmm." Jessica smiled meaningfully.

A few minutes later she and Sheffield were settled at a cozy, secluded table reading the dessert menu, while a strolling violinist serenaded them. Jessica felt as if she had stepped into a romantic movie.

"So tell me about yourself," Sheffield said when the cappuccino arrived. "I've heard a little bit about Elizabeth from Todd, but—" Sheffield paused. Jessica was tempted to quiz him about the Todd-Courtney story, but Sheffield's sorrowful tone made it sound as though the subject was closed. "But," he continued, "I know you can't take it for granted that twins are alike in every respect."

"Oh, no. We're not exactly alike," Jessica confirmed, her smile mischievous. "Just in the things that matter—beauty, brains, and so on!"

Sheffield laughed. "And so on?" he repeated. "I'm interested. Go on!"

Jessica filled him in on the basic details of her family and her life in general. Then she urged Sheffield to do the same. He listed his hobbies. "Tennis, though I was never very good at it. And sailing." Jessica nodded. Just what she wanted to hear—sailing, on the family yacht, no doubt, and tennis lessons with a private coach on the family courts!

"And I love traveling," Sheffield added. "Well, I already told you about the African trip. I won't bore you further about that."

"Oh, bore me!" Jessica begged. "I want to hear about all the places you've been."

"All right, but remember, you asked for it!" Sheffield warned good-naturedly. "I've spent a lot of time in Europe: France, Germany, Austria, Switzerland, Italy, Spain—you know, the grand tour. Plus I've been to Great Britain, the

Greek Islands, Japan, Australia, New Zealand, Bermuda, Brazil, and Mexico. The Soviet Union is next on my list."

"Wow." Jessica was breathless. "What a life. When do you have time for school?"

He laughed. "My parents only plan trips during vacations, of course. Traveling isn't the real business of life. I have lots of time for school and other important things."

"Such as?" Jessica prompted.

Just then their desserts arrived. Sheffield took a bite of his amaretto-flavored cheesecake and chewed it slowly before answering. "Sports and charitable work," he finally said.

"Charitable work?" Jessica wrinkled her nose as she sipped her cappuccino.

As Sheffield reeled off a list of popular causes, Jessica began to understand why he wanted to save the whales and feed hungry people all over the world. Really rich and famous people were always involved in some philanthropic scheme or other. Look at the Mellons and the Rockefellers. They had their names plastered over schools and charitable organizations nationwide. And all those big rock stars put on concerts to benefit something or other. It was obviously the thing to do.

Once you have more money than you could ever possibly spend, it's fashionable to donate some to charity! Jessica realized, eating a spoonful of gelato. *This charity business is just part of being an Eastman.*

Jessica pressed Sheffield for more details about his wealthy family. As he talked she caught herself yawning into her cappuccino once or twice. Was it possible that Sheffield Eastman was a little on the dull side? Jessica quickly decided it was just that Sheffield was so different from the boys she usually dated. Lovett Academy guys were bound to be more serious than the immature boys at Sweet Valley High.

On the sidewalk outside Venezia, Sheffield took Jessica's hand. "It's too early to take you home," he said, gazing down into her eyes. "It's a beautiful night for watching the moonlight on the water. How about a walk on the dock? I know where the marina is. Courtney's dad keeps his yacht there."

"That's a great idea," Jessica said enthusiastically. "I'm not in any rush to get home."

"Good." Sheffield ushered her around to the passenger side of the Mercedes and helped her into the car. Jessica felt like a princess stepping into a golden coach. She couldn't wait to get home and call Lila and tell her all about her date!

The usually busy marina was peaceful by night. Boats bobbed gently on the black water. Jessica and Sheffield strolled to the end of the dock and then stood silently for a few minutes, enjoying the night sounds—the soft lap of the waves and the creaking ropes.

"Beautiful, isn't it?" Sheffield murmured, putting an arm around Jessica's shoulders.

She leaned lightly against him. "Mmm. I love the water. I'm glad I'm not somebody who lives a thousand miles away from the ocean. I can't imagine living anywhere but in this area," she said softly.

"I know what you mean," he said. "It'll be strange to turn my back on all this next year."

"What are you talking about?" Jessica asked, puzzled.

"My semester off—my senior year project," he explained.

"That's right. You started to tell me something about it the other day," Jessica said, eager to learn more.

"Well, it's a little unusual." Sheffield smiled, keeping his eyes focused on the dark horizon. "Lots of kids petition for special senior projects, but mine's wilder than most!"

"What is it?" Jessica asked.

Sheffield shook his head. "The details aren't firm yet. I promise I'll tell you all about it when my petition's approved. Could be any day now!"

Jessica was disappointed, but as Sheffield bent his head to kiss her she decided she could definitely wait. They had done enough talking for the evening!

On Thursday afternoon Elizabeth experienced an unsettling sensation of déjà vu. Once again she was standing at the mailbox, and in her hand was an envelope from Todd.

But this time the return address was Sweet Valley, not Vermont. And instead of Todd's handwriting, the envelope appeared to have been addressed by a professional calligrapher. But the most important difference of all was that instead of "Miss Elizabeth Wakefield," the address read, "Miss Elizabeth Wakefield and Friend."

"And friend?" Elizabeth read out loud, staring at the envelope. That could mean only one thing: Todd expected her to bring a date to his party. In other words, he wasn't planning to ask her to be his date.

Elizabeth's eyes blurred with tears, and she sorted through the rest of the family's mail without really seeing it. "Lila was right," she whispered to herself as she stood on the front steps.

Todd *wasn't* waiting for Elizabeth. He had chosen Courtney over her. Courtney would be Todd's date at his big party.

Despite the heat of the sun on her bare arms, Elizabeth felt cold. The invitation was cold, she thought, slipping it out of the envelope before she entered the house. It was formal and elegant —raised black letters on creamy expensive paper. There was nothing Todd-like about it— nothing except his name, and even that didn't look quite the same in such fancy print.

She shut the front door behind her and walked down the hallway to the kitchen to drop the pile of mail on the counter. Then she headed up the stairs to her bedroom. As she passed

Jessica's door, Elizabeth yelled to make herself heard over the blasting stereo. "Jess, some mail for you!"

Jessica opened her door, revealing her messy room. "Thanks, Liz. Ooh, look! What's this?" Elizabeth watched as her twin tore open the invitation and scanned it quickly. "Wow, even Lila doesn't send out invitations like this!" Jessica raved. Then she noticed the tears in her twin's eyes. "Liz, what's the matter?"

Elizabeth held out her invitation for Jessica to see. Jessica glanced at it and shrugged. "Of course Todd invited you to the party, too. What's so upsetting about that?"

"Take a closer look," Elizabeth said in a tight voice.

Jessica studied the envelope again. Then her eyes widened. "Oh." Jessica nodded. "I see what you mean. 'And friend,' right?"

"Right," Elizabeth acknowledged, miserable. She wandered into Jessica's bedroom and collapsed on the unmade bed.

"Well, look." Jessica switched into what Elizabeth and the rest of the family called her cheerleader mode. "It doesn't have to mean what you think. See, mine says 'and friend,' too. Maybe the calligrapher put that on everybody's!"

Elizabeth shook her head. "I don't think so, Jess. But thanks for trying to make me feel better."

Jessica sat down on the bed next to Elizabeth. "I didn't succeed, though, did I?"

92

Elizabeth smiled halfheartedly. "Nope. Sorry."

"Well, you know what I think?" Jessica said brightly.

"What?"

"I think it's all for the best."

"How do you mean?" Elizabeth kicked off her sneakers and leaned back on the bed against the pile of pillows.

"Before, you were torn between Todd and Jeffrey, right?" Elizabeth nodded. "It was a total, terrible dilemma. It was ruining your life! Well, now your dilemma's over. Sure, maybe not in the way you'd expected, but it's *over*. And you love Jeffrey, don't you? You didn't want to break up with him."

"No, I guess I didn't," Elizabeth confirmed.

"So you should be happy!" Jessica exclaimed. "Now you get to stay with Jeffrey, the guy you love—and who loves you!"

Jessica was right. Jeffrey *was* the most wonderful boy in the world. Elizabeth knew she should be relieved and happy. *So how come I'm not?* she wondered.

Heedless of the fact that just yesterday she had been pulling for Todd, Jessica started listing Jeffrey's best qualities. Elizabeth listened tolerantly. Inside, though, she understood more clearly than ever before that she couldn't judge her feelings for another person by making a list.

But all that doesn't matter anymore, Elizabeth told herself as Jessica rambled on. *There's no more decision to make. There's no point in listening to my heart. Because*—Elizabeth felt sad as she recognized the truth—*when I listen to my heart, I know that it's Todd I love most.*

"And Jeffrey has the best legs, from playing all that soccer—" Jessica was interrupted by the telephone ringing. After a few moments of digging wildly under a pile of wrinkled clothes, Jessica unearthed her phone. "Hello?" she yelled.

Elizabeth jumped to turn down the volume on the stereo. Meanwhile, the blank expression on Jessica's face gave way to one of pleased excitement.

"Hi, how are you?" Jessica said into the receiver, her voice suddenly smooth. "I was hoping you'd call."

There were a few seconds of silence. Curious, Elizabeth watched her twin. After a moment Jessica smiled broadly and gave her the thumbs-up sign. "I'd love to! Eight o'clock sounds great. Bye."

Jessica slammed the phone down and then leapt straight into the air, flinging out her arms and shaking imaginary pom-poms. "Yee-*ha*!" she hollered.

Elizabeth burst out laughing. Sometimes her sister was too funny. "Who was that?"

" 'Who' is right! Make that *Who's Who*." Jessica collapsed on her bed, a smug smile on her face.

"Oh, let me guess. That was Sheffield Eastman, right?" Elizabeth asked.

"You got it," Jessica confirmed.

"Well?" Elizabeth prompted.

"*Well*, he just asked if he could *escort* me to Todd's party on Saturday! Lizzie, I'm the happiest girl in the world!"

Elizabeth laughed. She had lost count of the number of times Jessica had declared herself "the happiest girl in the world" because of some boy or other. "That's great, Jess," she said. "Sheffield did seem nice. And those *eyes*!"

"I know." Jessica's expression became rapturous. "Liz, he has everything. Seriously, he's the man I've been looking for all my life. He's handsome, he's rich, he's smart. And did you notice the cut of his sports jacket at that Lovett party? Definitely European."

Elizabeth couldn't help giggling. "European?"

Jessica knew Elizabeth was teasing her. She shook a finger at her twin. "Go ahead and laugh, Liz, but these things are important. You don't see anyone at Sweet Valley High wearing anything *half* that classy. Sheffield Eastman," Jessica said, savoring the name. "And to think I used to consider Bruce Patman a catch. Let me tell you, Liz, Sheffield's got everything Bruce does and *more*."

"Bruce Patman deluxe?" Elizabeth suggested.

Jessica nodded. "He could teach Bruce a thing or two. Sheffield has style, sophistication, sensitivity—"

"The three *S*'s," observed Elizabeth.

Jessica frowned. "Laugh all you like!" she said, her stern tone only causing Elizabeth's smile to widen. "You'll see. Sheffield's going to be the key to a wonderful future for me!"

As Jessica continued to daydream, Elizabeth slipped out of her sister's room, biting her lip to keep another tear from falling. The contrast was too painful. *Jessica's the happiest girl in the world. What about me?*

A wave of sadness washed over Elizabeth. She had just lost Todd for the second time in her life.

Ten

Jeffrey was knotting his new paisley tie when a car honked in the driveway. Slinging his navy blazer over his shoulder, he hurried outside. His car was in the garage, so they were going to Todd's party in Elizabeth's car.

Elizabeth smiled at him through the Fiat's window. "Lookin' good, French!"

"Well, let's get a look at *you*." He opened the door on the driver's side, and Elizabeth stepped out of the car.

Slipping off her loose jacket, Elizabeth twirled in a circle for Jeffrey's inspection. He whistled with approval at her royal-blue spaghetti-strap dress. "You'll be the prettiest girl at the party by a mile," he told her sincerely.

Jeffrey took the keys from Elizabeth and ushered her into the passenger seat. He backed the Fiat cautiously out of the driveway. "So," he said, making an effort to sound happy, "we're going to Lila's neighborhood, right?" Lila lived in the richest section of Sweet Valley, in the hills overlooking the town.

"Uh-huh," Elizabeth affirmed, turning her face away from Jeffrey to gaze out the window. "It's on the same drive." She gave him the exact address.

"OK," he said, stepping on the gas to scoot through a yellow light. "Should be easy to find."

Elizabeth nodded. This time her smile was visibly strained. Jeffrey smiled back, but his stomach felt queasy. *If only we were going somewhere else*, he thought. *A movie, the Dairi Burger, Miller's Point. Anywhere but Todd Wilkins's house!*

Jeffrey had spent more time with Elizabeth during the past week than he had at any point since Todd moved back to Sweet Valley. They had walked on the beach, talked on the phone a half dozen times, and done their homework together. On the surface it was like the old days, when Todd was still three thousand miles away in Vermont. When Elizabeth asked him to be her date for Todd's party, Jeffrey understood what that meant. He'd "won"—Elizabeth wasn't going to leave him for Todd. They would stay together.

But deep inside, a secret suspicion haunted

Jeffrey. He had heard the Todd-Courtney rumors just like everybody else at Sweet Valley High, and he couldn't help wondering if he had won Elizabeth's love by default because Todd had chosen someone else.

Elizabeth wasn't her usual self, that much was clear. She was affectionate and kind, but the sparkle was missing from her eyes. When Jeffrey held her in his arms, she didn't respond as warmly as she had in the past. She just didn't act like somebody who had made a choice and was happy with it.

Jeffrey rested his right hand on the back of Elizabeth's seat, behind her neck. He squeezed her shoulder gently. "This should be a fun party," he said, trying to convince himself. "I was talking to some of the guys at school yesterday, and it sounded like everybody plans to be there. Ken, Bruce, Aaron, Enid and Hugh, Winston and Maria, DeeDee and Bill . . ."

"My brother and Cara, too," Elizabeth added. "And Jessica and her date, Sheffield, from Cedar Springs."

"The band's supposed to be great," Jeffrey continued. "I'm ready to dance up a storm with you!"

"Me, too," Elizabeth said. But she couldn't have sounded less enthusiastic.

Elizabeth wanted to be Todd's date tonight, Jeffrey suddenly realized. He felt miserable as he turned the Fiat onto the drive leading up to Todd's house.

As they drove up the hill, they passed numerous estates. The houses, when you could even see them past the gates and high walls, were enormous.

Elizabeth clasped her hands tightly around her small black evening bag. She almost wanted to ask Jeffrey to turn the Fiat around and drive her home, she was so nervous.

Why am I even going to this stupid party? she asked herself. She hadn't seen or spoken to Todd since the day she received the party invitation, and she dreaded seeing him tonight. Most of all she dreaded seeing him with Courtney. But until she witnessed it herself, Elizabeth couldn't wholly believe that Todd was in love with someone else. A tiny illogical part of her was still hoping she was wrong about Todd's relationship with Courtney.

Elizabeth darted a look at Jeffrey's handsome profile. Tentatively she reached out a hand to touch his arm. She knew Jeffrey sensed something wasn't quite right between them. She had never been very good at pretending she was happy when she wasn't. But he continued to be patient with her, and she was grateful.

At the touch of her hand, Jeffrey turned and met Elizabeth's eyes, holding them for a brief but charged moment. "Here we are," he announced, swinging the Fiat through a set of ornate iron gates.

There were already a few dozen cars parked

along the long driveway. Jeffrey pulled up behind a glossy Mercedes sports coupe. He slammed his own door and then walked around to Elizabeth's side. "Madam, it would be my pleasure to promenade with you to yonder posh party," he drawled, offering his arm.

Elizabeth took it, her lips managing to approximate a smile. But her smile quickly faded as she and Jeffrey neared the house. This was Elizabeth's first visit to Todd's new home, and she felt like a complete stranger. It was all so imposing. The stately brick mansion was fronted by massive pillars. From a distant room the muted sounds of live rock music drifted out to the lawn.

Todd lives here? It was hard for Elizabeth to believe. She remembered his old house in Sweet Valley. It had been a homey, comfortable place. Elizabeth shook her head and clutched Jeffrey's arm more tightly. That house was part of the past. She had to face the present: Todd's new home and his new life—without her.

A few other newly arrived guests joined Elizabeth and Jeffrey at the door. They all entered the lofty front hall together.

And there was Todd, tall and handsome and looking like a movie star in a crisp white dinner jacket with a red carnation in his lapel.

Courtney Kane stood next to him. Her glossy mahogany hair was piled loosely on her head, held in place with glittering jeweled clips. She wore a strapless emerald satin gown that accentuated every curve of her body. A corsage of tiny white rosebuds garnished her slender wrist.

Jeffrey squeezed Elizabeth's hand, and together they approached their host and hostess.

Todd was greeting each guest with a hand-shake while Courtney made welcoming small talk. *I can't do it*, Elizabeth thought as she and Jeffrey faced Todd and his date. *I'd rather die.* But she held out her hand so that Todd could take it briefly in his own.

"Why, Elizabeth! How wonderful to see you again," Courtney cooed. "And who is this?"

Jeffrey shook Courtney's hand as Elizabeth introduced them. "Jeffrey, I'd like you to meet Courtney Kane," Elizabeth managed to say. "And you know Todd."

"Sure. Hi, Todd," Jeffrey said easily.

"Jeffrey." Todd's expression was completely blank. "I'm glad you could make it. Everyone's either in the ballroom or out on the patio that adjoins it. Just go down that hallway."

As she and Jeffrey moved on so that Todd and Courtney could chat with the next couple, Elizabeth's eyes met Todd's for a brief moment. The masklike smile, as painted and artificial as Elizabeth's own, did not leave his face.

What is he thinking? Elizabeth wondered, her heart pounding painfully. *Can he tell how much this hurts me? Does he care?*

Elizabeth fought the urge to run off and hide someplace where she could freely cry her heart out. But she wouldn't know where to find a bathroom in the enormous house, and if she had learned one thing lately, it was that crying wouldn't make her feel any better. Instead, still holding Jeffrey's hand, she followed him wordlessly down the long hallway to the crowded, noisy ballroom.

Eleven

The slow song ended with a poignant, lingering note. Gently releasing Elizabeth, Jeffrey sighed. For a brief instant he had a haunting feeling that he had just held her in his arms for the last time.

He was about to suggest another dance when his attention was diverted. Over Elizabeth's shoulder he had a fairly clear view through the french doors of the table at which they had been sitting on the patio. If he wasn't mistaken, that was Courtney Kane loitering by Elizabeth's chair. As Jeffrey watched, Courtney stuck what looked like a folded piece of paper in Elizabeth's jacket pocket. Then she glanced around in a very suspicious fashion, like a bad actress in a low-budget spy movie, and walked away.

That's weird, Jeffrey thought. *What is Courtney up to?*

It didn't make much sense. The only thing Courtney and Elizabeth had in common was Todd Wilkins, and Jeffrey couldn't picture Courtney writing Elizabeth to thank her for handing over her old boyfriend.

Just then Elizabeth touched Jeffrey's sleeve. "Jeffrey, I'm going to hunt up a bathroom," she announced, pushing the hair back from her forehead. She smiled wryly. "If I'm not back in half an hour, send a search party!"

"OK, Liz. Good luck!" The timing was just right, Jeffrey decided. While Elizabeth was gone, he would see if he could figure out what kind of game Courtney was playing. She didn't strike him as a particularly nice person. Whatever she wanted with Elizabeth, Jeffrey imagined it wasn't anything good.

After planting the note, Courtney headed back to the other end of the patio, where Todd was standing by the buffet table. It was easy for Jeffrey to follow her through the crowd without being noticed.

After saying a few words Jeffrey didn't quite catch, Courtney put a hand on Todd's arm and drew him away from the other guests.

Jeffrey followed Courtney and Todd through the semidarkness, beyond the glow cast by the Japanese lanterns hanging from the trees out back. Keeping out of sight, he came within earshot.

". . . a headache," Courtney was saying in a

feeble, pained voice. "It just came out of no-where."

"Maybe you should go inside and sit down for a while," Todd suggested, obviously concerned.

He put an arm around her, and she leaned against him. "It's just so noisy, even in the house." Courtney passed a trembling hand over her forehead.

Jeffrey, watching from the shelter of a palm tree, raised one eyebrow. If Courtney was putting on an act, she was pretty convincing. She really looked as if she were about to faint.

"I think I'd like to go to that cute little gazebo you showed me this afternoon." Courtney looked up beguilingly at Todd. "You know, just to lie down for a few minutes in the dark where it's quiet. I'm sure I'll feel better soon."

"If that's what you want."

"Would you help me there, Todd?" Courtney asked sweetly. "I'm not sure I remember the way."

Todd only hesitated for a moment. "Of course," he said. "It's on the west lawn. Are you sure you can make it?"

"I'll be all right," Courtney promised, continuing to lean against Todd as they turned their backs on the party and started toward the gazebo.

Jeffrey was certain that Courtney was up to something. She obviously had a plan—first the note and then the phony headache to get Todd to the summerhouse. But what was going on? And how did it involve Elizabeth? Giving Todd and Courtney a brief head start, Jeffrey followed at a safe distance.

"You're a fantastic dancer," Sheffield murmured into Jessica's hair. They were outside, but the tall windows of the ballroom were open, so the music drifted across the patio. Sheffield pulled Jessica closer as the band played another slow song.

"You, too," Jessica said, slipping her arms around his neck. Their dancing styles were definitely different. Jessica liked to get into the music and be wild, while Sheffield was more controlled and conservative. But what Jessica might have classified as a drawback in another boy she viewed tolerantly in Sheffield's case. His dancing complemented hers, she thought. That was it! They were wonderfully compatible. And Todd's party was turning into the most perfect night of her life.

As Sheffield danced her around the far side of the pool so they could steal a kiss beneath a breeze-ruffled palm tree, Jessica abandoned herself to the magic of the moment. Japanese lanterns twinkled among the palm fronds, competing with the clear light of the moon. And then there was Sheffield, at home in his elegant white dinner jacket. Clearly it wasn't rented; Jessica guessed he had a closetful of tuxedos. And she knew she looked sensational in the slim black strapless dress she had borrowed from Amy. Sheffield's eyes had practically popped out of his head when he came by the house to pick her up before the party.

The rock combo paused between songs. "How about a break?" Sheffield suggested, brushing Jessica's cheek with another kiss.

"A break sounds great," Jessica agreed. "I could go for a glass of punch!"

It was also a good time, she decided, to start mingling. While she and Sheffield had spent some time talking to the Lovett crowd, which included more good-looking, classy guys than Jessica had seen in one place in ages, she hadn't had a chance to flaunt him in front of *her* friends. And that was something she had been looking forward to ever since Sheffield had called to ask her to be his date.

What luck! Jessica thought as she noted that Lila, Bruce, Amy, and another half dozen or so of their Sweet Valley High classmates were clustered around the buffet table that had been set up on the patio. "Not only am I thirsty, I'm *starving!*" Jessica declared, taking Sheffield's hand firmly in her own. "Let's check out the buffet."

Once they reached the long, white-clothed table, however, Jessica walked right past the tempting finger food and elbowed her way into the circle of her friends, pulling Sheffield in with her.

"Why, hello, Lila." Jessica flashed Lila her brightest smile. "Hi, Drake. Good to see you again. Everybody, I'd like you to meet Sheffield Eastman. He lives in Cedar Springs, and he goes to Lovett Academy with Todd."

As Sheffield shook hands with the guys, Jessica smiled at the envious expression on Lila's face. She couldn't remember when she'd had so much fun showing her up! Drake Howard, whom Lila dated occasionally, was an attractive enough date. He *was* older—a sophomore at Sweet Valley College and a fraternity member— and that was a plus. But when all was said and done, he was still just another Sweet Valley boy. Jessica knew Lila had been trying to snag a Lovett guy for quite some time. That was why she was always kissing up to that revolting Courtney Kane.

"So, tell us about Lovett," Bruce asked Sheffield. "I've heard a lot about it, but I've never visited the campus."

Jessica could have kissed Bruce. This was just what she wanted—for Sheffield to talk about himself so she could rub in his superiority even more!

"It's a great place," Sheffield responded easily. "Beautiful old ivy-covered buildings, plus some interesting new architecture. I don't board because I live fairly close, but a lot of the kids do, and the residence halls have great parties, practically every night."

"I like the sound of that," Winston remarked.

"Could be my kind of school," Amy agreed, smiling.

"Well, it's not all play and no work," Sheffield told them. "The classes are pretty intense, and some of the teachers are really tough. But you get a great education."

Jessica nodded, feigning interest. She didn't feel like discussing the academics at Lovett. She wanted to turn the conversation around to Sheffield's family and their huge estate. That would really impress everyone!

A flash of inspiration hit her as she recalled her conversation with Sheffield about his plan to take time off from school. He hadn't told her exactly what it was all about, but he couldn't hold out in front of a whole audience of people. Jessica had no qualms about putting him on the spot. An international playboy-type story would really kill Lila.

"It sounds like you're going to be sorry to leave Lovett next year," Jessica said to Sheffield.

He looked down at her, slightly surprised. "Did I tell you about that?" he asked.

"You started to. And I'm dying to hear all the details!" Jessica encouraged him.

"Well, it's like this," Sheffield explained to the group. "Senior year at Lovett everybody has to write a special research paper. Up to fifty pages, on a topic that's independent from the rest of your classes. Most people just hang around the library and read a bunch of books, but I want to do something different, more active."

Jessica hung on to Sheffield's every word. The

rest of her friends appeared genuinely interested. Lila was pouting, looking from Sheffield to Drake with obvious dissatisfaction. *This is going to be even better than I expected!* Jessica thought gleefully.

"So I asked to take a semester off to do some special research for my thesis, and my proposal was just approved!" he announced excitedly.

Jessica beamed. Sheffield would probably be spending the semester touring the medieval cathedrals of Europe . . . trading bonds on the floor of the New York Stock Exchange . . . climbing Mount Everest . . .

"What does your project involve?" asked Ken.

Jessica held her breath. She kept her eyes trained on Lila's face. This was one reaction she didn't want to miss!

"Well, for a while now I've really been thinking about my life-style and privileges," Sheffield began. "I have everything I need to be comfortable, and a lot more. But there are a lot of people who aren't nearly so fortunate. I've been volunteering occasionally at a homeless shelter in Santa Barbara, and next year I'll be living there and working full-time."

It took a moment for Sheffield's words to sink into Jessica's brain. She watched as Lila's pout changed to a look of amusement. A homeless shelter! *What?* Jessica turned and stared disbelievingly at Sheffield.

"It will be sort of like sociological fieldwork," he continued earnestly. "I think it's important to understand as much as possible what it's like to be needy, so that you can help people more effectively. I really want to immerse myself in this experience—shed the trappings of wealth, you know? My Mercedes is for sale, and I'll be donating the money to charity, if anyone's looking to buy a car!"

His Mercedes? That gorgeous midnight blue car in which she arrived at the party? Jessica just kept staring at Sheffield. How could he do this to her?

Lila was the one gloating now. She practically laughed out loud at Jessica's flabbergasted expression.

In order to save what face she had left, Jessica knew she had to pretend *this* was the plan she was so excited about. But it was hard, when she wanted to scream and throw a cup of punch in Sheffield's well-meaning face—and another one at Lila.

"That's a really neat thing to do, Sheffield," Aaron said. "I respect you for taking action like that. It takes a lot of guts to get out there and help tackle such a big problem."

"You're so *noble*," Lila cooed. "Jessica didn't tell us you were such a *saint*."

Sheffield laughed. "I'm no saint," he assured Lila, putting an arm around Jessica's waist. "I just feel I have a duty to society, that's all."

Jessica forced herself to smile. She felt like the wife of a political candidate, who had to support her husband even when he sounded like an idiot. "It's a great project," she managed to croak. *Change the subject, somebody, quick!* she prayed.

Fortunately, Ken and Winston started joking about who was going to be the first person that night to end up in the pool, jacket, tie, and all.

"You're such a champion swimmer these days, Egbert," Ken teased Winston, referring to a recent school field trip. Winston and Jessica had fallen overboard when their small lifeboat capsized in a fierce storm. "Show us your best stroke!"

"Nope, I'm staying dry. You'll be the winner of the wet tuxedo contest, not me!" Winston predicted genially.

Winston and Ken began to wrestle. They moved closer and closer to the edge of the pool, for a minute teetering dangerously on the slick tiles. With a devilish grin Bruce stepped up and gave them the necessary push. There were a couple of yells, and then there was a gigantic splash as Winston and Ken fell into the pool.

The crowd by the pool resounded with laughter. As Ken and Winston began to perform a hilariously clumsy water ballet routine, Winston's girlfriend, Maria Santelli, kicked off her shoes and jumped in after them. A few more adventurous souls leapt into the lighted pool, and soon the noise of splashing and shouting was almost louder than the band.

Sheffield chuckled, his bright blue eyes twinkling. Jessica was the only person who was not amused. Her date was still the best-looking guy at the party, but all of a sudden he didn't look nearly as much like Prince Charming to her as he had a few minutes earlier.

They were standing close to the pool's edge. Jessica placed a hand on Sheffield's arm. It was very, *very* tempting! But with tremendous self-control she resisted the urge to push Sheffield into the water—project and all!

Twelve

Elizabeth stood in front of the ornately framed mirror in the huge downstairs powder room, studying her face. She looked pale and tired.

Another hour and Jeffrey and I can leave without offending anyone, Elizabeth told herself glumly as she put a hand into the pocket of her jacket, which she had retrieved before heading for the bathroom. She touched the small comb she had brought along—and felt something else.

Elizabeth pulled out a piece of white country club memo paper, folded into a small, neat triangle. Unfolding it curiously, she discovered a hastily printed note, addressed to her.

Dear Elizabeth,

I'm waiting for you in the gazebo. I need to talk to you—it's very important. Will you meet me here, as soon as possible?

The gazebo is at the far side of the west lawn in the orange grove. You can't miss it.
Todd

Elizabeth stared at the note. The thought flitted through her mind that Todd never printed, but it was gone an instant later as she reread the note. Todd wanted to see her and talk to her. What did it mean?

Despite herself, despite everything, Elizabeth felt her spirits rising joyfully. What could he have to say to her that was so important?

Maybe, just maybe, things aren't over between us after all! Elizabeth thought. *Maybe Todd's had a change of heart. Maybe he just realized that Courtney isn't the girl he wants to be with.*

Elizabeth was surprised by how much she wanted that to be true. She couldn't hide the truth from herself any longer. Elizabeth loved Todd, as much as she ever had. She wanted them to be together again.

Just then there was an impatient knock at the door. "Just a sec!" Elizabeth called, running the comb rapidly through her hair.

"Liz?" a voice queried.

"Jess?" Elizabeth opened the door, and they both burst out laughing.

"I was starting to think whoever was in here was taking up permanent residence!" Jessica exclaimed.

"Well, I would've been out a while ago, but . . ." Elizabeth stopped, unable to explain.

Jessica shot an eagle-eyed look at her sister. Then she noticed the piece of paper Elizabeth was still clutching. Before Elizabeth could slip the note back into her pocket, Jessica snatched it away from her. "What's *this*?" Jessica squealed. She didn't wait for Elizabeth's permission to read it. "Todd—the gazebo—Liz, what's going on?"

Elizabeth plucked the note from Jessica's fingers. "I don't know. And I'm not sure I'm going to find out."

Jessica pushed her twin back into the powder room and latched the door securely behind them. "Listen, Liz," she lectured sternly. "A word from the wise. Don't meet Todd!"

Elizabeth was surprised at Jessica's vehemence. "Why not?" she asked.

"Just take it from me!" Jessica rolled her eyes. "These private-school boys aren't all they're cracked up to be! Todd probably just wants to tell you he's going to abandon his new wealth, sell his BMW, and drop out of society, like Sheffield!"

"What?" Elizabeth was totally bewildered. "Jessica, what are you talking about?"

"I'll explain later," Jessica promised. She opened the powder room door and shoved Elizabeth out. "Now I need a little privacy, please!"

The door clicked shut, and Elizabeth shook her head, mystified. She walked slowly and thoughtfully back toward the ballroom. She wanted to meet Todd—she had to. But she wouldn't sneak off behind Jeffrey's back.

I'll show Jeffrey the note, Elizabeth decided. *I'll tell him I'm going to talk to Todd to find out if things are really over between us.* Elizabeth knew it wouldn't be easy to tell Jeffrey she still cared about her ex-boyfriend. But she had to do it. Eager to get the scene over with, she stepped through the ballroom's doors, out onto the patio. Breathlessly she scanned the crowd for her date. But Jeffrey wasn't at their table. In fact, he was nowhere in sight.

Elizabeth spent a few frantic minutes hunting for him, but with no luck. With every second that passed, her desire to see Todd, with or without Jeffrey's consent, grew. Finally she knew she couldn't hold back any longer.

As they crossed the dark, deserted west lawn, Todd was barely aware of Courtney's presence, even though he held an arm firmly around her waist. He was sorry she didn't feel well, but he had only listened with half an ear as she described her symptoms. He was happy to walk her to the gazebo. It didn't much matter what he did with his time when Elizabeth belonged to another guy.

Courtney stumbled and gasped. "I caught my heel in the grass," she apologized. "Twisted my ankle a bit." Now she was leaning so heavily against Todd that he was practically carrying

118

her. Her head was on his shoulder, and her silky hair tickled his neck.

The gazebo loomed up in front of them, nestled in a grove of orange trees. The fragrance of orange blossoms hung in the air. "It's a romantic spot, isn't it?" breathed Courtney, her voice barely more than a husky whisper.

It *was* romantic. Todd had thought so the first time he saw it. An airy gazebo with cushioned benches inside—just right for a midnight tryst. But Todd had fantasized about being there with Elizabeth, not Courtney.

"I'll see you inside," he told Courtney in a clipped tone. "Then I really should get back to the party."

"That's fine," she said. "Thanks for the escort, Todd. I'm feeling better already."

They stepped together into the gazebo, Courtney still clinging to Todd. Inside, she turned to face him, her body pressing close.

Todd had been going through the motions of helping Courtney, as though he were in a dream. But all of a sudden, once they were entirely alone, Courtney became very real and immediate. Instead of frail and weak, she was passionate. Her slender arms twined around his neck, and she lifted her full lips to his. Todd didn't have a chance to pull away and tell Courtney that this wasn't what he wanted. Her warm mouth had found his, and they were kissing.

*   *   *

119

Rounding the west side of the mansion, Elizabeth peered across the lawn in the moonlight. Against the dark line of trees she detected the shape of a small building. The gazebo!

She ran over the grass, her heels sinking deeply into the soft turf with each step. She was too eager to see Todd to go slowly.

The blossoms of the orange trees surrounding the gazebo were pale in the moonlight as Elizabeth approached. She saw a shadowy figure within. It was Todd!

Then her racing heart lurched to a momentary stop. The shadowy figure inside was really *two* figures—Todd and Courtney, locked in a passionate embrace.

For a moment Elizabeth stood rooted to the spot. *How could Todd do this to me?* she wondered, putting a hand to her throat. *Was this what he had to tell me that was so important?*

She took a deep breath, trying to be fair and rational despite her hurt. *Todd couldn't have meant for things to turn out this way,* she thought, desperate for an explanation. *Maybe he really did intend to apologize and let me down gently so my feelings wouldn't be too badly hurt. Then Courtney came along and, well, one thing led to another. After all, it's Courtney Todd loves now.*

Elizabeth turned, the crumpled note falling from her numb fingers. Tears streamed down her face as she hurried away.

Elizabeth couldn't bring herself to return to the party. She ran from the joyful sounds of laughter, music, and conversation. Finding the Fiat in the line of parked cars, she jumped inside. She fumbled in her jacket pocket for the key and then started the engine with a roar.

Still crying, Elizabeth sped down the driveway away from Todd's house.

Thirteen

Not far from the gazebo, Jeffrey paused. He had seen Todd and Courtney enter the secluded structure, and now seemed like a good moment to head back to the party. He knew Elizabeth would be looking for him, and he was also curious to see what sort of note Courtney had left for her. It seemed pretty clear that Courtney had lured Todd to the gazebo for a romantic interlude. But what did the note have to do with it? Jeffrey wondered.

Quietly he turned on his heel and began walking back toward the house. He had only taken three steps when he halted again. Somebody was hurrying across the dark lawn toward the gazebo.

Jeffrey was momentarily amused. *This is some*

party! he thought. Then with a jolt he recognized the slim figure. It was Elizabeth.

Standing in the shadows, Jeffrey was fairly sure he was invisible. Elizabeth didn't appear to see him, but she *did* see something in the gazebo that stopped her in her tracks. An instant later she whirled around and fled back the way she had come.

It happened quickly, but not so quickly that Jeffrey didn't get a glimpse of the expression on Elizabeth's face. Even in the dark the shock and the tears were unmistakable.

Jeffrey pushed his hands deep into the front pockets of his gray trousers, his head spinning. Just what was going on here? The note in Elizabeth's jacket. Courtney's suspicious headache. The gazebo. *The note!*

Something white had slipped from Elizabeth's hand before she raced away. Jeffrey ran to the spot as quietly as possible and picked it up. It *was* a note, signed by Todd. But Jeffrey would have bet a year's allowance that Todd didn't write it or know anything about it. Courtney must have faked the handwriting as well as the headache.

The sound of low voices at the gazebo brought Jeffrey back to the present. He didn't want to be caught lurking in the bushes, but he didn't have time to bolt back to the patio. As Todd and Courtney emerged from the gazebo, Jeffrey took a giant step backward and pressed himself against the scaly trunk of a tall palm. Courtney and Todd passed within a few yards of his hiding place, but neither noticed him. They were obviously absorbed in their own separate thoughts. Courtney's smile was triumphant, while Todd looked confused, almost miserable.

You don't have to be a genius to put the pieces of this puzzle together, Jeffrey thought, shaking his head. Todd wasn't wild for Courtney, as the rumors had it. But Courtney clearly was going after Todd. The whole note and headache business looked to Jeffrey like a clever ploy to alienate Elizabeth so that Courtney could have Todd for herself.

Jeffrey kicked at a tuft of grass as he walked slowly back toward the party. The puzzle was whole now, the picture was clear.

Elizabeth hadn't yet confessed to him that she still cared for Todd. Now she didn't have to. Her face a few moments ago, full of misery and despair, spoke for itself. Jeffrey had been right when he thought that maybe Elizabeth was just staying with him because Todd wasn't available. Now, by all appearances, Todd *wasn't* committed to Courtney. And chances were that Todd's heart still belonged to Elizabeth, just as hers did to him.

Jeffrey stopped at the far end of the patio. He scanned the happy faces in the crowd until he found one as tense and preoccupied as his own—Todd's.

Now I'm the one who has to make a choice, Jeffrey realized. Jeffrey knew whom he loved. Elizabeth was the most important person in his life, and he would do anything to keep her. And he *could* keep her—by staying quiet about what he'd seen. She and Todd would never know how Courtney Kane had manipulated them.

But I'd know, Jeffrey thought, heaving a troubled sigh. He knew he would pay for it every day, every time he was with Elizabeth. In order to have her all to himself, Jeffrey would have to shoulder a heavy load of guilt.

He could keep quiet and feel guilty, or he could tell Todd the truth about Courtney's scheming, and risk losing Elizabeth forever.

Jeffrey pictured the girl who had come to mean the world to him. Elizabeth . . . sometimes serious, sometimes laughing, always caring, beautiful, and unique. Jeffrey hadn't really known what love was until he met Elizabeth. Together they had shared something rare and rewarding. They looked out for each other, trusted each other. Elizabeth had never let him down.

And I can't let her down now. . . . Jeffrey's throat ached with unshed tears. *In the end, if I really love her, isn't it her happiness that's most important?* he asked himself.

Jeffrey straightened his broad shoulders and took a deep breath. He walked purposefully across the patio, dodging enthusiastic dancers.

Todd was filling two glasses with punch while a fully recovered Courtney stood safely out of earshot, chatting with a couple of people.

Jeffrey tapped Todd on the shoulder. When Todd turned around, his eyes registered surprise. "Hi, Jeffrey," he said politely.

"Todd, can I talk to you for a minute?" Jeffrey asked.

Elizabeth yanked hard on the steering wheel, pulling the Fiat back onto the road. That was the second time she had let the car drift over onto the right shoulder.

"Get a grip, Wakefield!" she lectured herself, wiping a stray tear off her cheek with a shaky hand.

For fifteen minutes Elizabeth had been driving like an unthinking robot, turning down streets at random. She didn't know or care where she was going. She only wanted to leave Todd's party and her heartache behind.

Now she blinked, for the first time focusing on a street sign: Secca Lake, 1½ Miles.

"Secca Lake," Elizabeth read aloud. Funny she should end up heading in that direction. The tree-fringed lake was a favorite recreational spot in Sweet Valley. There was swimming, boating and an area for picnickers. Once upon a time it had also been Elizabeth and Todd's favorite romantic retreat.

Tonight Secca Lake was deserted. Elizabeth

turned into the small parking lot at the south end of the lake where the public swimming area and picnic tables were located. At the end of the lot, she nosed the car onto an unpaved road. The lane ran halfway around Secca Lake, ending at an abandoned boathouse. It was strictly off-limits, but she and Todd had ventured down it many nights. The lakeside clearing by the old boathouse was a peaceful, private spot, perfect for talking and kissing.

Elizabeth pulled the car up next to the boathouse, facing the lake, and cut the engine. For a long moment she sat like a statue, her hands gripping the steering wheel so tightly, her knuckles ached. One tear raced down her cheek, then another. Soon Elizabeth was sobbing.

After a full five minutes of crying, Elizabeth rooted in the glove compartment for the package of tissues she kept there. After drying her face and neck, she blew her nose. Then she undid her seat belt and stepped out of the car.

Elizabeth peeled off her shoes and stockings and tucked them behind the driver's seat. Then she picked her way over the pebbly shore and, disregarding the delicate fabric of her dress, climbed onto a broad, flat rock by the lake and sat down. She hugged her knees with her arms.

The surface of the lake was as smooth and still as glass, broken only by a shimmering silver trail of moonbeams. The silence was profound. After a few minutes Elizabeth's breathing evened out, and the tight feeling in her chest eased. As the beauty and peace of the night wrapped around her, little by little the stormy clouds lifted from her mind.

In the lakeside stillness, Elizabeth was able at last to hear her heart, loud and clear. Now she knew with calm certainty that despite her strong feelings for Jeffrey, Todd was the one she really loved.

I've been so unfair to Jeffrey, Elizabeth recognized sadly. She tossed a pebble into the lake and listened as it entered the water with a small, muffled sound. It wasn't right to stay with him when she could no longer give him her whole heart. She had to break up with Jeffrey. Maybe someday they could be friends again, maybe not. But she couldn't go on living a lie. As for Todd . . .

Elizabeth stared out over the lake. If Courtney was his choice, so be it. She couldn't make him change his mind or convince him to give their love another chance. That was a decision he had to come to on his own, just as she had.

Elizabeth bent her head and rested one cheek on her knees. All of a sudden she felt tired, and old. This had to be the longest night she had ever lived through! But morning would come—it always did. *I'll be all right,* she thought, sad but confident.

Just then Elizabeth was startled by the noise of another car. She stood up abruptly, her heart thudding nervously. The car's headlights were flickering through the trees bordering on the lake as it drove closer to her.

Someone else knows about this little spot. If it's a couple looking for privacy, I'd better make myself scarce. Elizabeth started to return to the Fiat just as the other car entered the clearing. Then she froze in mid-stride. It was Todd's new BMW!

Fourteen

Todd braked to a stop and cut the engine. He jumped out of the car and rushed toward Elizabeth.

"Todd!" she cried, stunned.

"I knew I'd find you here!" he exclaimed, hoarse with relief. "Oh, Elizabeth . . ."

Elizabeth didn't know whether to laugh or cry. Before she had a chance to do either, Todd had taken her in his arms.

For a long minute they stood holding each other tightly. It felt good, after such a long time of refraining from any expression of affection. Even though Elizabeth didn't know what had happened to bring Todd to Secca Lake, the love in his eyes and his embrace was unmistakable.

At last Elizabeth pulled back from him. "What's going on?" she asked. "Did you leave your party? Courtney . . . ?"

"Jeffrey told me everything," Todd explained. "I drove past your house, but your car wasn't there. I just had a feeling you might be at our spot by the lake. Instinct, I guess."

"Jeffrey," Elizabeth repeated, confused. "What did Jeffrey tell you?"

"I'd better start at the beginning," Todd said. He put an arm around Elizabeth's shoulders, and together they walked toward the shore. "Let's sit down."

Just moments before, Elizabeth had been sitting by herself on the rock, feeling lonelier than she ever had in her whole life. Now Todd was sitting beside her. It was like a dream come true, and her head was spinning.

"Where does Jeffrey come into the story?" she prompted.

Todd took one of Elizabeth's hands and held it while he talked. "At the party Jeffrey came up to me and told me something he'd discovered by accident about Courtney—and you and me."

While Elizabeth listened Todd related as much as he knew of what Courtney had done and how Jeffrey had discovered her treachery.

"You mean the note? You didn't write it?" Elizabeth asked.

Todd shook his head. "Courtney must have written it and then pretended she didn't feel well. She timed it just right, knowing you'd come by the gazebo and see us. . . ." His voice trailed off; he was embarrassed. Elizabeth dropped her eyes as the pain of that scene came back to her. "I know how it looked, Liz," Todd said softly. "Courtney kissed me, and, well, I guess I let her. I wasn't thinking. I mean, I *was* thinking, but not about her. I was thinking about you, and how miserable I was without you."

Elizabeth looked up at Todd again. "You mean you're not in love with Courtney?"

Todd laughed. "Not even close! When I first met her, I thought she was fun. A little shallow, but good company. And our parents have been pushing us to spend time together. But, Liz, I was never interested in Courtney *that* way. It was only after I heard about the ring Jeffrey gave you and how serious you were becoming that I asked Courtney to the party. I thought you'd made your choice and it wasn't me."

"Ring? What ring?" Elizabeth asked blankly. As Todd repeated the story he had heard from Sheffield about her and Jeffrey, Elizabeth remembered a similar incident: Lila Fowler, by the Wakefields' pool, feeding *her* details of Todd's supposed relationship with Courtney. Suddenly it all made sense.

Elizabeth and Todd traded rumors and then shared a rueful laugh. "Well, I've got to say this for Courtney—she sure was thorough," Elizabeth observed.

"Thoroughly cruel and dishonest," Todd added bitterly. "After I talked to Jeffrey, I confronted Courtney. She tried to play dumb, but I'd listened to her lies for the last time. I just left her, and the party!" He grinned. "Great host, huh?"

Elizabeth had been nestled in the crook of Todd's arm. Now she sat up and pulled away from him slightly. *Jeffrey*, she thought. *Todd and I wouldn't be together at this moment if it weren't for Jeffrey!* He had been the one to figure out what Courtney had done. Then he'd shared the truth with Todd, even though he must have known he might be sending Todd straight into Elizabeth's arms. It was a brave, generous, and unselfish thing to do. Elizabeth's throat ached, the tears threatening once again. Jeffrey had done many sweet things for her over the course of their relationship, but this last gesture was perhaps the sweetest of all.

Elizabeth turned to look up at Todd. He was watching her face with a tender expression, as if he understood what she was thinking. Lifting a hand, he gently brushed a stray wisp of hair back from her forehead. "I couldn't wait until tomorrow to straighten this out," Todd said. "I couldn't leave you thinking I didn't care. Because I do care, Liz. I never stopped."

Elizabeth smiled brightly. "I really feel like I'm having some kind of crazy dream, Todd. Not too long ago it seemed as if my world had turned upside down. I've been spinning in circles ever since I first heard your family was moving back to Sweet Valley. I was so torn. And then just as I started to think that I might want to give our love another chance, I thought you'd fallen for Courtney." Laughing, Elizabeth shook her head. "For once my life was more mixed-up than Jessica's!"

"Are you still—mixed-up?" Todd asked, his eyes anxious.

"No." Elizabeth shook her head. "I think I know myself and my heart better now than I ever have."

"And what does your heart think about us?"

In answer Elizabeth put her hands on Todd's shoulders and tipped her face to his for a kiss.

Later they sat close together in happy silence. Todd gently stroked Elizabeth's hair. "You should probably be getting back to your party," she whispered.

Todd sighed. "You're right. Everybody must be wondering what happened to me! And I still have to take care of the band and the caterers," he remembered. "But I could spend the rest of my life right here with you."

"We'll be back," she promised, leaning close to kiss him again.

They agreed to drive in tandem back to Todd's house. Elizabeth knew she had to find Jeffrey. It was time for them to talk honestly about the situation.

Before climbing into his car, Todd put his arms around Elizabeth one last time. "I can't believe I'm touching you!" he marveled. "Right now I really feel like I'm *home*, for the first time since I came back to California. It's almost as if I never even went away."

Elizabeth shared Todd's joy completely. But there were still a few small worries lingering in the back of her mind. "It can't be exactly the same as before," she reminded him gently. "Lovett Academy's a long way from Sweet Valley High, in more ways than one. You're part of a whole new world. Are you sure there's room for me?"

"Are you crazy?" Todd hugged Elizabeth again. "Going to Lovett hasn't changed me or the way I feel about you, and it won't! Ever! How much money my dad makes, where I live— none of that's important. You have to believe me, Liz."

"I do," Elizabeth assured him. At that moment she did believe it with all her heart. She and Todd had shared the past and conquered the obstacles of the present. Their future together started tomorrow.

And it could be—would be—even better than their past.

Is everything rosy in Elizabeth and Todd's future? Find out in Sweet Valley High #59, **IN LOVE AGAIN.**

NOW

SWEET VALLEY HIGH®

IS A GAME!

- **RACE THROUGH THE HALLS OF SWEET VALLEY HIGH**
  - **MEET SWEET VALLEY'S MOST POPULAR GUYS**
  - **GO ON 4 SUPER DREAM DATES**

You and your friends are students at Sweet Valley High! You can be Jessica, Elizabeth, Lila or Enid and go on a dream date. Live the excitement of the Junior Prom, or go to a Sweet Sixteen Party. You can go surfing or join the bike tour. Whatever you choose, be sure to watch out for the other girls. To keep you from winning, they might even steal your boyfriend.

YOU'LL FIND THIS
GREAT MILTON BRADLEY GAME
AT TOY STORES AND BOOK STORES
NEAR YOU!

Prices and availability subject to change without notice

Buy them at your local bookstore or use this page to order.

- -

Bantam Books, Dept. SVH7, 414 East Golf Road, Des Plaines, IL 60016

Please send me the books I have checked above. I am enclosing $_____
(please add $2.00 to cover postage and handling). Send check or money
order—no cash or C.O.D.s please.

Mr/Ms _____

Address _____

City/State _____ Zip _____

SVH7—6/89

Please allow four to six weeks for delivery. This offer expires 12/89.

YOUR OWN

SLAM BOOK!

If you've read *Slambook Fever*, Sweet Valley High #48, you know that slam books are the rage at Sweet Valley High. Now *you* can have a slam book of your own! Make up your own categories, such as "Biggest Jock" or "Best Looking," and have your friends fill in the rest! There's a four-page calendar, horoscopes and questions most asked by Sweet Valley readers with answers from Elizabeth and Jessica

It's a must for SWEET VALLEY fans!

☐ 05496 **FRANCINE PASCAL'S SWEET VALLEY HIGH SLAM BOOK**
Laurie Pascal Wenk   **$3.95**
